He laughed, and this time she did not turn her head away fast enough, and she saw his laugh, like the curve of the moon. A pale crescent of evil amusement. What have I done? she thought, wanting the wind to come up, the sun to rise.

"Dawn is nearly here," he murmured. He gestured with a finger like foil toward the pink beginning of a new day. "Go to school, my dear. It will begin."

"What will?"

"Being popular, of course. Isn't that what you wanted?" His words were whispery as the wind. His skin, the color of mushrooms, faded into the dawn. His black drapery vanished among the hemlocks. The air stayed thick and swampy where he had stood.

With difficulty she drew a breath.

You did what you had to do, she told herself. And it wasn't so bad.

Also by Caroline B. Cooney

THE VAMPIRE'S PROMISE #1
DEADLY OFFER

CAROLINE B. COONEY

SCHOLASTIC INC.

New York Toronto London Auckland Sydney
Mexico City New Delhi Hong Kong Buenos Aires

ISBN 0-439-55395-4

Copyright © 1991 by Caroline B. Cooney

All rights reserved.
Published by Scholastic Inc, 557 Broadway,
New York, NY 10012.
SCHOLASTIC and associated logos are trademarks
and/or registered trademarks of Scholastic Inc.

12 11 10 9 8 7 6 5 4 3 2   3 4 5 6 7 8/0

Printed in the U.S.A.
First Scholastic printing, June 1991

Originally titled *The Cheerleader*

THE VAMPIRE'S PROMISE #1
DEADLY OFFER

Chapter 1

"Suppose," it said in its voice like antique silk, faded and slightly torn, "that I could make you popular."

It did not smile, for which Althea was glad. She did not particularly want to see it smiling. She waited, but no explanations followed. Talking to it was somewhat upsetting. Althea kept her back to the wall, waiting for it to leave. Usually it left rather early, having, she supposed, appointments to keep. Tonight it stayed. Waiting. She knew it could always wait longer than she could.

Her heart snagged on that word *popular*. At last Althea asked, "How could you make me popular?"

It nodded for some time, its entire trunk pulsing slowly back and forth, as if it were on a spring. "Tell me," it said, in that slippery satin voice, "what is the most popular group in school?"

That was easy. "Cheerleaders," said Althea with yearning. The Varsity Squad was a closed unit of slim blonds and sparkly brunettes who not only never spoke to Althea, but, far worse, had never noticed her, either.

"Who," it went on like a river or a tide, "do you wish had never gotten on the squad?"

That, too, was easy. "Celeste," said Althea. Celeste had made Varsity as a freshman, which, to the sophomores, juniors, and seniors who failed to make it, seemed unfair. Celeste was quite extraordinarily beautiful. At first Celeste did not appear sufficiently energetic to cheer. She walked slowly, languidly, hands trailing. Celeste seemed more a romantic dreamer than a screaming, leaping, possibly even perspiring, member of a gymnastics-oriented squad. But cheerleading transformed her. Once in uniform, Celeste became a star.

And popular. *So popular.*

Althea longed for the popularity that cheerleading brought.

Althea was a gentle girl. She had sweet features and a demure posture. When she spoke, people quieted to hear her distinctive whispery tremor. In elementary and middle school, Althea had had a circle of giggly girlfriends, a phone that rang constantly, invitations every weekend to spend the night, or order pizza, or go to the movies. She was on the softball team, won several silver ribbons in horseback riding, and went on a wonderful group skiing trip. She had thought that at high school she would become a serious skier, and she had bought a beautiful ski outfit to shine on the snow.

But high school was horrible.

The circle of friends, like a kaleidoscope turned and refocused, had split cleanly apart, to form new groups. One group was heavily into Individuality and New Experiences; they wore trendy clothing or torn jeans, unique sweatshirts or obscene earrings. They found Althea altogether too dull to bother with. Another group had boyfriends, and Althea, without one, was unwelcome. The third group became scholarly and embarked on a soul-whipping routine of trying to beat one another out with exam grades and extra-credit reports.

Althea's throaty whisper became a liability. Nobody heard it. She had to raise her voice, and the voice felt foreign: like an intruder, like a stranger yelling.

Loneliness absorbed her life.

It was a quiet life: no phones, no laughter, no gossip, no giggles.

It was November: a month of dark and chill.

A month in which Althea saw herself, like an abandoned waif in the gutter, without hope.

"Perhaps," the voice continued, "Celeste could be taken off the squad."

She slipped down those words, as if on a water-slide at an amusement park. She noticed how the voice liked to split sentences, teasing with the first word: who . . . what . . . perhaps . . .

She did not like standing quite so close. It had given her all sorts of assurances, but did she know, for sure, that she could believe these promises? Under the circumstances?

"Would there not," it continued, in a lazy, inquiring sort of manner, as if they had all year to consider it, "be tryouts for Celeste's replacement?"

Althea nodded. The cheerleading squad was a precision team. They worked in pairs. They would have to have an even number. Althea had had years of dancing and gymnastics. Nevertheless she had not made the team.

The high school was jammed with girls who had had years of dancing and gymnastics. "There would be a lot of competition," said Althea, remembering the taste of humiliation and despair when she had been cut from the list long before the final round of tryouts.

"Perhaps . . ." the voice said, with such slowness that it seemed to be melting away, "I could arrange for the competition to be missing."

She let her mind drift over that. Skimming like a seabird on the surface of the suggestion. Not landing, no. Not part of it . . . but thinking about it. The power of it. The potential of it.

What a change it would make in her life! She would be among the lovelier, more exciting girls. The girls who partied and laughed, drove fast cars, and sat with adorable boys.

Me, Althea thought. Popular. A cheerleader.

"Perhaps someday I would even be captain," she whispered.

"Perhaps so." Its skin was the color of mushrooms.

"And date somebody on the basketball team," she breathed, imagining it. She remembered how the cheerleading squad sat on the bus with the team, how if they won the game there was laughter, and shared snacks, and a favorite CD was played while they foot-danced, because the bus driver didn't allow standing. How in the back of the bus, girls sat entwined with their boyfriends, their laughter quieter, more intimate. How couples got off the bus last, holding hands.

"Maybe even Michael," said Althea, so softly she was not sure she had let the thought out, because the thought was so precious. *Michael*.

"Maybe even Michael," the voice agreed.

Althea pulled herself together. She was envious of the popular girls, but she was kind. She didn't want anything nasty to happen. And Celeste seemed like a perfectly nice person. "What would you *do* to Celeste?" said Althea warily.

It smiled. The teeth were not quite as pointed as Althea had expected, but she shuddered anyway.

She was told, with an air of reproach, "It doesn't hurt, you know. It's just rather tiring. Celeste would simply be . . . rather . . . tuckered out."

The eyes changed their focus, leaving Althea's face. She felt as if she were released from suction cups.

It stared at the sky, at the black cloudless sky sprinkled with stars, gleaming with moonlight. It seemed to find a companion with whom smiles were exchanged. "Celeste would be back in school the next day."

"Then why wouldn't she stay on the squad?"

"I told you. She'll be tired. She'll feel a need to resign. She'll want a little time to herself. There's no cause for you to worry. Her grades won't suffer."

Althea decided not to think about the details.

She did not let herself think about being popular.

I can't condone . . . but on the other hand . . . a simple exercise that would leave Celeste . . . well . . . tired . . . and after all, Celeste is only a ninth-grader, and I'm in tenth . . . and I deserve it more. . . .

Its fingernails were gray, like foil.

"Althea," it said, stroking her name, feeding it new ideas, "think about school tomorrow. Think how you sit alone at lunch. How nobody talks to you in study hall. How nobody shares a soda with you after class."

How vivid it was. How often it had been true.

The voice was thready and sticky, like a spider's web. "But if you're a cheerleader . . ."

Althea saw herself among the slender blonds and sparkly brunettes.

"You, Althea," said the voice, softer than clouds, "you deliver Celeste."

Althea shivered.

"I," breathed the vampire, "will make you popular."

Chapter 2

But how? How was this supposed to work?

Celeste wafted down the halls of high school like a sunset of spun gold, wrapped in the possession of her friends. From a distance Althea would see that soft hair, those sparkling eyes. From around a corner Althea would hear that trembly laugh, a laugh that shivered with delight.

It was so unfair! Celeste had every beauty, every friend, every power.

You deliver Celeste. I will make you popular.

My only claim to popularity, thought Althea, is that I have the same lunch schedule as the cheerleading crowd. I get to stand in the same cafeteria line.

When Althea went to lunch, Celeste was ahead of her, shimmering like a mirage. Celeste skimmed through the line, putting almost nothing on her tray, gliding to her seat. Celeste's laugh sparkled across a crowded table, where friends jostled and squeezed.

Althea's tray was heavy, and the plates slid around, bumping one another and threatening to spill. She carried it carefully, and when she finished paying, looked around for a place to sit. A group of girls she knew fairly well filled a distant table; there was no room. A girl like Celeste could dance up and they would make room, but for a girl like Althea they did not.

Her old friends from middle school were with their new friends from other parts of town. If she joined them, she would be a river barge shoving through sailboats. They would part to let her through, but she could never join. The only thing worse than being alone was to have people tolerate you because they felt pity.

Althea's eyes swept the entire cafeteria, and in the entire cafeteria there did not seem to be an empty seat.

"Come on," said an impatient voice behind her. "Get going."

Althea lifted her heavy tray and took two steps out into the hostile lunchroom. People trotted past, their trays as full as hers, but their steps were light. They found places to sit, and people looked up and said to them, "Hey, how are ya? Sit down!"

There is no room for me, thought Althea. There never will be.

She walked past table after table, and from each chair eyes turned, inspected Althea, and turned away. Every student in the high school had a chance to say, "Sit with us." Every student in the high school said nothing. Eventually Althea was back at the counter. If she had had any appetite, it was gone. She sat her tray down, untouched.

I'll just stand outside in the courtyard till lunch is over, Althea thought. I'll pretend —

A silver shot of laughter came from the cheerleaders' table. Celeste planted a sweet kiss on the cheek of the handsome boy next to her.

I want that life, Althea thought. I want to laugh and kiss and have friends! But how do I invite her to my house? The closest I'm ever going to get is the same building.

The second day was worse than the first, for Althea could not find the courage to enter the cafeteria at all, but brought a bag lunch and sat on a bench outside, pretending she liked the outdoors, pretending she needed the fresh breezes in her hair in order to compose her thoughts.

Lies, all lies.

On the third day, she forced herself into the cafeteria again. She did not actually get in the lunch line. She drifted on the edges, trying to think of a strategy.

Cheerleaders, thought Althea, important people, jocks, the party crowd — they're always on another side of the room, sitting at a different table, laughing at a different joke. There's no way to cross that dividing line. Either you're popular or you aren't.

Her heart filled with longing to be special, the

way they were. She inched closer to hear their affectionate, silly talk.

Althea paused next to Celeste's table, pretending her attention was caught by something beyond, an interesting tableau, perhaps, of dieticians and cooks. In the cafeteria, she was camouflaged like an animal in the jungle, merely another anonymous student passing by to get extra ketchup or another dessert. They paid no attention to Althea. They just rattled on about their cars.

It seemed that Ryan's car had only one working door out of four and that to get in and out, you had to use the rear right passenger door. (Althea imagined herself in the crowd, giggling as she doubled over to squeeze in the back, crawling over boys' legs, gear stick, and parking brake to reach the front seat.)

It seemed that Kimmie-Jo had backed her new car into a tree. The car's trunk now had an interesting configuration, along with a tree print. (Althea imagined herself in the car with Kimmie-Jo when it happened, screaming, "What will your parents say? You're dead, Kimmie-Jo!", giggling, and suggesting they go to Dairy Queen and have ice cream first, and *then* deal with Kimmie-Jo's parents.)

Michael, however, had a car that was not only new to *him,* it was actually new. His father had bought it for his seventeenth birthday present last week. How like Michael, thought Althea, staring with adoration, forgetting to pretend she was neither watching nor listening.

Celeste said sadly, "I'm only fourteen. I won't be able to drive my own car forever and ever and ever."

Althea's heart hardened. I'm sixteen, and I have nothing! thought Althea.

"That's okay," said Michael, smiling at Celeste. "We'll give you a ride when you need one."

He had such a fine smile. Brotherly, welcoming — and yet sexy. He smiled like that at ninth-grader Celeste! For no reason except that Celeste was on Varsity Cheerleading!

Althea walked straight into the group.

She expected to feel the prickles of their distaste, to have Kimmie-Jo and Michael and Ryan and Celeste look at her with amazement. An intruder. A pushy unwanted nobody.

But Ryan said, "Hi, Althea. How are you?"

Ryan knew her name? She was stunned. "Fine, thank you," she said.

"You live in that huge spooky house at the bottom of the hill, don't you?" said Celeste. Celeste shuddered pleasurably. Her pretty golden hair quivered, and the boys smiled gently at her. "They say it's haunted. Have you ever seen ghosts, Althea?"

Althea did not like to lie. "I have never seen a ghost," she said carefully.

"Your house isn't haunted?" said Celeste, with evident disappointment.

"Of course not." Althea sensed the group getting ready to move. They were always in transit, these popular people, drifting like a flock of bright-feathered birds from one perch to another. She needed to hold on to them. Or, at least, on to Celeste. She made a quick offering. A dangerous offering, because it trembled on the edge of truth. But it was all Althea had. "We do have a Shuttered Room, though."

"What does that mean?" Celeste had a pretty, little giggle and a trick of biting her lower lip as she giggled, taking her breath in funny little snatches. The boys looked on adoringly.

"There's a room in the attic," Althea explained. "The circular tower. You may have seen it when you've driven by. The tower room has three windows, none of which are ever opened. There are shutters on the inside of the windows and shutters on the outside."

"What's the room for?" asked Michael.

"It's for staying away from."

"Oh, wow," said Celeste, entirely satisfied. "I knew that house was haunted."

"It is not haunted," said Althea rather sharply. "It's simply that nobody is supposed to enter the Shuttered Room."

"What happens when somebody does?" asked Michael.

She paused.

She had an answer to that now, of course. For she, a month ago, had done just that. Against all rules, against all tradition, she had touched the shutters. And now she knew what happened.

If you were to open the inside shutters, you would hear a whistling gurgle, the sound of somebody struggling for air, the sound of a living person in a locked coffin.

If you were to open the outside shutters, the wind would whirl into the tower, and the tower air would whirl out, and in the exchange of old air for new, something passed, something changed.

The vampire was set free.

She did not know where he came from: inside the tower or outside. She did not know where he stayed: inside the tower or outside. But the shutters were the key to his prison — and he was the key to hers.

The vampire could set Althea free. Free from the hostile cafeteria, free from loneliness. *You give me Celeste, and I will give you popularity.*

Althea fastened her eyes on Celeste. Althea's whispery tremor, deep in her throat, sounded frightening and mysterious. "Nobody ever has. It's a family tradition. The shutters in the Shuttered Room stay shuttered." She smiled, first at Celeste, then at Michael.

The kids laughed, repeating the rule like a tongue twister. *Susie sells seashells on the seashore. The shutters in the Shuttered Room stay shuttered.*

The bell rang, and the kids dispersed, as even popular groups must, for class or gym or art or library. Michael strode blithely alone down the hall, headed for something special, no doubt; he could not possibly take dull repetitive classes the way she had to. Ryan was bouncier; he lunged in the other direction, as if he had athletic records to set. Kimmie-Jo was sultry, stunning, the way she always was, sitting, walking, or cheering. Becky, another cheerleader, popped out of a classroom door, and Becky and Kimmie-Jo hugged with that relaxed affection popular people show each other. Unpopular people who did that would just be pathetic.

Althea caught up to Celeste and walked on with her. Think companionable thoughts, Althea told herself. Don't let Celeste see through you. Say something normal. "You know which one my house is," Althea said, "but I don't know where you live."

Celeste made a face. Even pouting, she was very pretty. "Way out of town, Althea. Miles and miles. I hate living there. I can never go anywhere unless somebody's willing to drive me. They're always willing the first time, but they make that trip once and they're not so willing a second time."

She's confiding in me, Althea thought. She's treating me like a friend.

Maybe she would not have to deliver Celeste to the vampire after all! She and Celeste would become friends, and that would be the door through which Althea entered popularity.

"Ryan came once, and after that, he's just been 'busy.'" Celeste sighed deeply, very sorry for herself. "And Becky — well, she came once, and when I asked her to drive me again, she frowned and said my parents would have to bring me to the party."

Had *she* been asked to a party of Becky's, Althea would have slogged across swamps and swum rivers. She was supposed to feel sorry for Celeste, all because Celeste had to get party transportation from relatives? "That's rough," said Althea sympathetically.

"And you heard Michael say he'd drive me, but he's dating Constance, of course, and I can hardly ask him to pick up Constance first and then come for me."

So Michael was dating Constance. Constance was one of those overwhelming people who was simply brilliant at simply everything. There was not an activity in which she did not shine, not a subject in which she was not a scholar, not a sport in which she did not excel. Constance was lovely and willowy, strong and interesting, funny and sweet.

Of course Michael was dating Constance.

Althea was exhausted by the mere thought of Constance.

Celeste gave several more examples of how unpleasant it was to live so many miles out in the country. It became increasingly difficult to grieve for somebody who had been asked to three events last weekend and could get transportation to just two of them.

"After school today," said Althea, "would you like to come over to my house?"

Celeste gave Althea a dazzling, sparkling smile. It was a smile on a par with Michael's: a world-class welcome of a smile. Althea warmed inside, forgave Celeste for whining, and thought of friendship.

"You're so sweet, Althea," said Celeste. "That's so nice of you. But I have cheerleading practice, of course."

Chapter 3

After school Althea did not go home. She drove around town in a jealous rage. Street after street passed beneath her tires, like some great black, bleak grid of life.

If only Celeste had not said *of course*!

It was that *of course* that was the knife in the back.

A light turned yellow, and in her present mood she wanted to slam down the accelerator, roar through the intersection, leave a patch on the pavement, and fill the faces of bystanders with foul exhaust.

But she drove carefully, as she had been taught. Then, like lightning filling the sky with sheets of silver, she remembered something: Celeste was too young to drive. *But Althea was not.*

I have a license. And a car. Why, I'd be happy to drive Celeste home. Or to a party. Or anywhere else that Celeste might choose. Briefly, anyway. Until . . .

. . . well . . .

And *of course*, after that, Celeste would be too tired. It wouldn't matter anyhow.

You have cheerleading practice, of course, thought Althea. Celeste, my friend, I have a car, of course. And a Shuttered Room, of course. And a vampire.

Althea turned left. Then right. She gripped the steering wheel like the compass of life. Three miles and she was back in the school parking lot.

Beyond the buildings and the tennis courts, the football team was practicing. Boys were lined up on each side of the field, hurling themselves at one another. From that distance it was impossible to tell which heavily padded body was which.

The school had many ells and additions. Althea circled the building, looking for cheerleading practice.

The grass had just been mowed, and the air smelled wonderful, like hay and countryside.

She remembered the vampire's smell. When he did whatever he did, would Celeste notice the smell first, or would she — ?

Stop! thought Althea. Don't think about the details.

Around the next brick wall was a small paved courtyard, and there they were, all twelve of them.

Mrs. Roundman, their coach, was not pleased. "Not even half trying!" she was shouting. "Not one of you! You are all so lazy! What is cheerleading — an activity for melted marshmallows? You act as if you'd run out of energy spreading peanut butter on bread! Call yourselves cheerleaders? Ha!"

Several girls were close to tears. Several seemed merely irritated, as if they had better things to do than stand around while Mrs. Roundman had a temper tantrum. And one was amused.

Mrs. Roundman did not miss this. "Celeste?" she bellowed. "You think this is a joke, perhaps?"

"No," said Celeste, trying to smother her laugh. "Of course not, Mrs. Roundman."

Althea caught Celeste's eye and giggled.

Celeste giggled back like a coconspirator.

Or a friend.

I should give her another chance, Althea thought. We could be good friends, I know we could, I can tell by the way she's sharing that giggle with me.

"One more chance," said Mrs. Roundman grimly to her squad. "I said every leg is to reach the same height on the kick, and that's what I meant."

Quite a few other people were watching practice. Two squad members' boyfriends were leaning against a brick wall, playing cards. A boy Althea did not know was doing his chemistry. His glasses had slid down his nose, and he looked sweet and childish. Three ninth-grade girls looked at their favorite cheerleaders with open adoration. A little knot of kids was sharing a single soda and monitoring one another's swallows.

She would have liked to join the card game. Help with the chemistry. Sip the soda. Even join the ninth-graders.

But after the first brief glance her way, nobody looked at Althea again.

The cheerleaders worked hard. Kimmie-Jo had the most style, and Celeste was the most beautiful, but Becky gave off an air of joyful celebration. While the other girls were breathless from exertion, Becky seemed breathless from love of cheerleading.

Finally Mrs. Roundman ended practice and stalked off. Althea did not know what she could be grumpy about. In Althea's eyes, the squad was perfect.

Celeste, out of breath and pink-cheeked, dropped to the ground next to Althea. "She's a bear," confided Celeste.

This is what friendship is, Althea thought. Somebody telling you something they wouldn't tell somebody else. "I can see. Does she always treat you that way?"

"Or worse. Honestly, I don't know where they find these coaches!"

Althea thought Mrs. Roundman was an excellent coach. Certainly the school had the best cheerleaders Althea had ever seen. But she said sympathetically, "Gosh, you must be tired, Celeste."

"I'm utterly exhausted. People don't know how difficult cheerleading is. You don't get the credit you deserve." Celeste arched her back like a cat and slowly melted down. A few golden threads of hair across her forehead annoyed her, and she stroked them into place. Rotating her long neck to relax herself, she added, "And what's more, I have to wait an hour for a ride home. A whole hour! Just sitting here! Till my parents are out of work and can come for me."

What a lovely neck she has, Althea thought. It really is swanlike, just the way they say a high-fashion model's should be. What soft white skin she has.

Since we're becoming friends, Althea thought, perhaps I'll ask her if she has ever thought about modeling. I've always wanted to be a model myself. We could go into the city together!

"I am so bored," said Celeste.

Althea looked at her uncertainly.

"*Nobody* is around," Celeste said. "Everybody has left."

Not quite everybody, thought Althea. I'm here.

Celeste ran beautifully polished fingers through her silken hair. Her nails were pale, pale pink.

But they could get paler, Althea thought. And I know somebody who would also think that's a lovely neck. "You poor thing," said Althea. "Well, I'm heading out right now. Want a ride?"

Chapter 4

His skin had darkened in patches, like fruit going bad. If she touched it, the skin would feel like a sponge. The fingernails seemed detached. She could pluck them, harvest them, fill a basket with old vampire nails.

Althea closed her eyes to block out the sight, and then quickly opened them. It was difficult to breathe evenly in his presence, but she knew that if her breathing were ragged and frightened he would enjoy it; it would give him power over her. So she regulated her breathing. She blocked out visions of Celeste being touched by the vampire's spongy skin, his foul mold against her swan-sweet neck, his smell in her hair. But she had to know. "What happened?" said Althea.

The vampire looked surprised. "You want details?" His teeth overhung his lower lip, shimmering like pearls, like Celeste's hair.

"I don't want details," said Althea hastily. "Just — well — an overall picture."

With a long bony finger, the vampire traced his lips, as if savoring something. How thin his lips were. How bloodless. Although actually he looked somewhat healthier than the last time Althea had encountered him.

Althea felt a little queasy. What could have made him healthy?

I did it, she thought. I actually gave a vampire his victim.

The air around her thickened. It crawled up her legs and crowded against her spine, and her heart, and her head. She could not see the air, but she could feel it, all woolly and damp, whispering, *That's what you did. You are bad, you are evil, Althea.*

She straightened her back and stiffened her jaw. I did what I had to, she thought. And Celeste deserved it. So there.

The dark drapery that seemed to be the vampire's clothing shifted and swirled as if it were leaving. But the vampire stood still. The hem of his black cloth blew toward Althea. She stepped back, and the black cloth reached farther, trembling eagerly. The vampire collected it back and wrapped it around himself like a container. To Althea he said, "It was only necessary for Celeste to enter the path of my control. Once you and she circled the house, she was within my light path."

"Light? You are dark. You are night."

"It is in fact a dark path," admitted the vampire. "I thought you would better understand a comparison to the rays of the sun." He smiled again, his teeth the only bright thing on earth, those notched glittering fangs that — Celeste had known.

Had it hurt? Had Celeste understood? Had Celeste talked to the vampire? Did she know who had led her into the dark path?

Althea looked off to the side. It was dark this early in the morning. Frost sparkled on the ground. The hemlocks and firs were black as night. The moon was still visible. Stars trembled. There was no wind. The world lay quietly in the shadowy circle of the house and the trees.

"I was able," said the vampire, his voice as wet and muggy as a swamp, "to migrate within Celeste's boundaries."

To migrate. It sounded like swallows and robins. It sounded rather pretty and graceful, an annual event.

She was very relieved. She had thought the word would be puncture, or stab, or even gnaw. But migration. That was peaceful. Perhaps Celeste had not even noticed.

Yesterday, Celeste had stayed on to have a Coke. Had admired Althea's bedroom. Shivered at the spookiness of the Shuttered Room. When Althea drove Celeste home, Celeste had chattered about school, about boys and clothes. Celeste had not sounded like a girl caught in a dark path.

The black cloth escaped from the vampire's twisted fingernails. Little threads from a frayed edge spun toward her, like a spider's web, hoping to snag her. The fringe wove itself into more cloth, and grew in Althea's direction.

Althea said slowly, "Am I in your dark path?"

"No. There are some people who are unreachable."

He reached me pretty well, thought Althea. I gave him Celeste. What if she knows? What if she says so in school? What if she tells people?

"You opened the shutters, Althea. You and I, we are evenly matched. We are both in control, and both of us may go only so far. But Celeste, I fear, is in a different category." He did not look as if he feared a thing. Or ever had. It was not fear that lined his lips, but hunger.

I'm not in control, Althea thought. If I were in control, I would have made myself popular the day high school began.

"So, after midnight," said the vampire, his voice wafting past like fragrance, the sound of his pleasure like perfume, "I visited Celeste."

Althea looked quickly down at the ground. It swayed. Or Althea did.

She reached out for something on which to steady herself, but the only object near her was the vampire. She yanked her arm back and shoved both hands in her jeans' pockets. Then she spread her feet for a firmer stance. She was glad to be wearing a heavy jacket. Maybe they were evenly matched, but a few extra layers of protection would not hurt. She adjusted the collar on the jacket. Tucked it under her hair. Zipped the fat silvery zipper up to her chin.

The vampire laughed, and this time she did not turn her head away fast enough, and she saw his laugh, like the curve of the moon. A pale crescent of evil amusement. What have I done? she thought, wanting the wind to come up, the sun to rise.

The black drapery flew out behind him, like bat wings. He pulled the cloth back and went on laughing.

Her breath felt stale and used. It seemed to Althea that her own breath was her soul, rising up a sad and lesser thing than it had been.

"Dawn is nearly here," murmured the vampire. He gestured with a finger like foil toward the pink beginning of a new day. "Go to school, my dear. It will begin."

"What will?"

"Being popular, of course. Isn't that what you wanted?" His words were as whispery as the wind. His skin, the color of mushrooms, faded into the dawn. His black drapery vanished among the hemlocks. The air stayed thick and swampy where he had stood.

With difficulty she drew a breath. She tasted him and spat the air out, walking backward, covering her mouth, until she was near the garden where the air was fresher.

In the house, she had little appetite for breakfast. You did what you had to do, she told herself.

And it wasn't so bad. Celeste's just going to be tired. And you — you get to be popular!

For so many months Althea had entered high school with her eyes lowered, her posture caved in, to keep from having to see that nobody saw her. Today she walked with eyes lowered and posture caved in because . . . *if they do look at me . . . will they know what I've done . . . who it is that I talk to in the dark . . . what I gave him?*

"Althea!" cried a girlish happy voice.

Althea spun around as if being attacked.

"Althea, I love your hair like that," said Becky gaily, catching up to Althea. "It's all fluffy and kind of — I don't know — sparkly."

Becky. The best cheerleader. The one Althea most wanted to be liked by, and to be like!

Althea wet her lips with nervousness. "I was out early this morning," she admitted. "The mist probably settled on my hair."

"Up early?" asked Becky. "I'm always up early, too. That's so neat to meet somebody else who does that. See, my parents always go for a prebreakfast run, down to the lake and back. Their circuit is five miles." Becky beamed joyously. "Lots of times I go with them."

How demented, Althea thought. Running five miles on purpose, when you could be lying in bed? Althea struggled to return Becky's exuberant smile.

"And why were you up early?" Becky asked.

Althea tried to think of an explanation, but nothing came to mind. "I really like the stars and the night sky," said Althea. It sounded very lame. Even more so than running five miles.

She had scarcely noticed that they had been joined by Ryan. She was dumbfounded when Ryan said, "No kidding! I took astronomy last year, Althea, and I really got into it. You know that the night sky changes continually, so that the constellation you could find in March is not the same as the one you find in November."

"You and your constellations," said Becky indulgently. She gave Ryan a friendly poke. He tugged her ponytail back. "Althea doesn't care about that, Ryan."

"I'd like to learn," said Althea. "I'm really quite ignorant. I just sort of go outdoors and stare upward. I don't know anything, really."

"Do you have a telescope?" asked Ryan seriously.

It had never crossed Althea's mind to want a telescope.

"Because that tower room in your attic would be such an excellent location," said Ryan. "I mean, you're in a really dark part of town."

If he knew how dark, he wouldn't be so eager, Althea thought.

"No streetlights," said Ryan, "no lights from all-night car dealerships, nothing to spoil your view of the stars." He smiled at her. He said, "I have a tele-scope you could learn on."

He's suggesting that he could come over! Ryan! Ryan of the football team! At my house!

Becky, bored by stars, said, "Did you get that al-gebra, Althea? I thought it was really hard."

Althea had forgotten that she and Becky were both in second-year algebra. Of course they never sat near each other. Becky sat with another cheer-leader named Dusty. Normal people could not have nicknames like Dusty. They would get teased until they actually became dust, or lint, or other under-foot objects. Only a cheerleader could say out loud, with pride, "My name's Dusty."

Ryan said, "I could bring my telescope over. We could put it in the tower room."

"The tower room," Althea repeated. Her hair prickled. No, no, no! She could not ever have any-body in the tower room. The vampire was free, his dark path lit.

"The one with all the shutters," Ryan explained, as if Althea were not familiar with it.

"Wouldn't it be neat to have a slumber party in that tower room?" Becky cried.

Althea could not think. A slumber party. Oh, how she wanted to have a slumber party! A dozen girls all at her house, all laughing and happy and glad to be there.

But the tower room?

Becky locked arms with Althea. Together they

headed for algebra. Ryan trailed after them, talking about telescopes and stars. Far down the hall Michael waved, smiling. Althea felt her popularity rising on that wave.

Becky said, "We don't have cheerleading practice today. You want to come over to my house, Althea?" Becky plopped down on the first available seat — not her usual seat near Dusty. "I mean, first we'll go to Mickie D's, of course, and meet everybody, but then we could go over to my house." She yanked Althea down next to her. Becky got a teasing, provocative look on her face. "Ryan lives next door," she said, as if making an offering. "We could play telescope together."

Ryan heaved a great sigh. He had followed them into algebra. Althea was confused. Ryan didn't have algebra. He was a year older. He had trigonometry. Why was he accompanying them here?

"My telescope, Becky," said Ryan, although he was facing Althea, "is not a toy. Although I am sure Althea and I can think of plenty of games to play." He winked at Althea.

Ryan had winked at her. Michael had waved at her. Becky had sat with her. Althea didn't care what had happened to Celeste. She would never care. She winked back at Ryan.

"You're sick, Ryan," said Becky. "Get out of here, you're annoying the algebra class. Go to your silly trig."

Ryan grinned. "I'm not sick," he told Althea.

"I'm a very interesting person. So. Are you coming to Mickie D's, Althea?"

She nodded, and he nodded back, and that was heaven. She burned with joy; she felt like a house on fire. When the algebra teacher called on her, she had the right answer; and when Becky made a joke, she had a quick laugh.

I'm here, thought Althea. I'm where I deserve to be.

Among friends.

Chapter 5

But before McDonald's came music.

Chorus was another high school group that had not turned out the way Althea had expected. She was one of sixteen altos. She had not made friends. She yearned to sit between two girls, both of whom would talk to her; instead she sat on the end of a row, sticking out into the room, next to one girl who never turned her way. Sitting on the end gave her a good view of the curved sections and the friendships other people had made.

I could sit in the middle, she thought. With a popular alto on my left and a cute baritone on my right. She steeled herself. She moved sideways over bookbags and shoes. She said to the alto, "Mind if I sit here?"

The alto beamed at Althea. "Sure! That'll be a nice change."

And Dusty, whose seat it usually was, said, "Oh,

good, I'm sick of being suffocated in the middle of the pack. Thanks, Althea."

She sat in the center. One of the crowd. The laughter and chat wrapped her up like a blanket hot from the dryer. She giggled with the boy on her right. He said, "I'm really sorry, but I don't know your name."

"Althea."

"What a neat name. I never heard it before." He smiled. "Althea," he repeated.

Before she could ask his name, the music director whacked the top of his stand with his long white stick and, in his martial-arts way, began warm-up exercises.

How special her voice sounded from the middle. Being an alto wrapped her in companionship; the boy's voice an octave lower added a dimension to singing she had never known. For the first time that year, the director met her eye, smiled, and nodded at her.

She felt like an opera star.

The director cut them off. In the silence before he gave more orders, Celeste entered the music room. Her sparkling eyes were dull. Her golden hair was limp.

There were three steps down because the room was designed for tiers of singers or instrumentalists. Celeste stood at the top. She shifted her load of books to her other side for better balance. Celeste felt her way down one step, panted slightly, and rested before taking the next step.

"You're late," said the music director sharply.

"I'm sorry." Celeste looked foggy. "I've felt sort of slow today."

"I am not interested in excuses," said the director irritably. "You are late. I do not tolerate lateness."

Celeste shuffled down another step.

The boy next to Althea muttered, "This is a cheerleader? No wonder we don't win any games." He rolled his eyes as Celeste tried to focus on the final step down. "Want a cane?" he said cruelly.

Althea no longer wanted to know the boy's name. She no longer wanted to know her own name. What have I done? she thought. Celeste was just supposed to be a little bit tired. She hardly even looks alive!

Althea tried to breathe for Celeste, to suck in rich clear oxygen that would energize her. But Celeste did not breathe deeply. Celeste stumbled and dropped her books.

The music director sighed hugely, exaggerating patience with this idiot who could not even cross a room. The girl who took attendance said dryly, "While we're waiting, Celeste, I'll make announcements. Think you can find the soprano section by then?"

If that were me, thought Althea, I'd blush scarlet. But Celeste is just shuffling on.

Then Althea herself went white as paste.

Celeste was not blushing. How could she?

To blush, you needed blood.

* * *

Becky laughed with intense excitement, as if she and Althea were going on a grand expedition, instead of just to McDonald's. Twisting and turning, Becky told every giddy detail of her day. Her black hair was pulled tightly back into a ponytail, and with every syllable, every move, seemingly every thought, both Becky and her ponytail bounced.

Althea tried to concentrate on what Becky was saying, to realize that she was going to McDonald's with the crowd, but she kept seeing Celeste's shoe inching toward the edge of the last step, trying to find bottom.

"Lighten up!" Becky commanded her.

As if it were orders from a general, Althea obeyed.

It was only two miles to McDonald's, and yet, by the time they were in the parking lot, Althea was younger, happier, and noisier. She, too, bounced out of the car. She, too, jumped up and down clapping as Ryan drove in to join them.

Ryan had been joined by a boy named Scottie, whom Althea hardly knew. It was a treat to see these two muscular young men get out of Ryan's car. First, Scottie dove over the seat back, landing like a beached whale half on the floor and half on the seat. Then, lumbering to his knees, head thrust forward, he opened the right rear door. This door, too, had its problems. Scottie emerged very carefully.

"Hey!" shouted Ryan, diving over after Scottie. "Don't close that door on my face."

"Oh," said Scottie. "Well, I guess I could wait another second or two. But I'm a fast-track kind of guy. I don't like to hang around, Ryan."

Ryan slid out. First, one long jeans-wrapped leg. Then an arm, a broad chest, a dark and handsome head of hair, and finally the other leg.

Althea had intended to daydream of Michael, but now she found herself encompassed by Ryan. Ryan was a weight lifter who talked of how many pounds he could bench press, and he knew all his muscles by name.

Everybody had a cheeseburger except Ryan, who ordered three Big Macs. He ate each in only four bites, his teeth dividing each huge burger like pie.

"Well, that's what's new in my life," Becky said, wrapping up a discussion Althea had missed while admiring Ryan's eating habits and muscles. "Althea, your turn to talk. Hold up your end of the conversation. What's new in your life?"

Ryan, Becky, and Scottie waited. They went on swallowing milk shakes. Waiting to hear what was new in her life.

What's new in my life? thought Althea. I've gotten to know a vampire quite well. His skin is the color of mushrooms. I don't know how he gets in touch with me. What do you think of Celeste, in her altered state? Do you know that I did that? This girl with whom you are having a cheeseburger — she hands people over to vampires?

Ryan and Scottie frowned slightly. Becky looked irritated.

Althea struggled to think of things to talk about. Had anything happened in class? After school? Had she gone shopping? Or even cleaned her room?

It seemed to Althea that, except for the vampire, she had no life.

Suddenly, to her horror, the vampire was standing there. Her throat closed up. Her eyes glazed.

He's not here! she thought. He can't come into a McDonald's! Certainly not in broad daylight. This is not fair. The backyard is one thing, but —

She opened her eyes.

He was not there.

Her nerves had fabricated him.

She breathed again, and realized to her shame that the solitary sigh was her only contribution to the conversation around her.

Becky giggled. "Well, that was exciting, Althea," she said. "We must chat about this again one day."

"Don't pick on her," said Ryan. "You're so mean, Becky."

"She's not mean," said Althea quickly. "I'm slow."

Ryan took this opportunity to discuss his telescope. Weight lifting was his daytime activity; stars were his nighttime activity. Scottie took this opportunity to mention several things that normal teenage boys enjoyed doing at night, as opposed to something lame and pitiful like studying satellite orbits.

"Here's what I say," said Becky. "I say we have a party at Althea's, because it's new, and we haven't partied there, and I'm sick of all the old places. Ryan can set up his telescope in that tower room, while we dance on those big old porches."

Althea's smile trembled. She had fulfilled her obligation to the vampire. She could do as she pleased. And yet . . . she had not shut the shutters. Was he still there? Where was that dark path, exactly? Could he touch other people? Would Becky . . . ?

Althea's body was rigid, as if her blood had stopped circulating — or been drained. "I don't know if that would work out, Becky. I mean, I'd love to, but —"

"All right, all right," said Becky, sulkily. "I just think it's somebody else's turn, is all. It seems to me the parties are always at my house."

"That's because your parents let you do anything all the time, Becky," Ryan said. "Most people's parents never let them do anything." He stuffed his napkins into his cup, stuffed his cup into his burger box, and squashed the whole thing into a remarkably small square. "So, what's Celeste's problem?" he said to Becky.

Althea's stomach knotted up. This was it. This was where they found out, where they understood, where they caught her!

Becky shrugged. "She didn't want to talk. Said she was tired."

"She stumbled around the school today like a zombie," said Scottie.

"She could at least have been polite," said Becky. "Here she is, a ninth-grader, everybody on the squad has been very nice to her, and she couldn't even be bothered to let us in on her problem. I asked her if I could help and she shrugged. That did it, that shrug. You can't have secrets from your teammates. They don't like it."

"Let's not talk about Celeste," said Ryan. "Let's talk about you."

He meant her. Althea. Ryan wanted to talk about Althea. An uncertain, joyous smile began on her lips. Ryan said, "Come on, more. More." He touched her lip corner with his finger and drew the corner up till Althea laughed out loud.

Celeste won't be tired long, Althea thought. She'll perk up in a few days. I'm not going to worry.

Anyway, it's worth it.

Chapter 6

How dark the yard was.

Althea had not known such darkness existed in the world. There was not a hint of light. Nothing at all that was less than black. And yet she could see where the vampire was and where he wasn't.

He was half in the hemlocks. Indeed, he seemed half hemlock. His arms were among the needled branches; his hair might have been growing straight from the trees.

"You wanted me?" he said. "How flattering. You want to give a report, perhaps? Tell me how things are going with your new popularity, perhaps? It isn't necessary, my dear. Since I created this popularity, I know exactly how it is going."

She had thought he was part of the shutters, that the tower room was his coffin, that his tomb was the house. But no. He was growing out of the trees, the thick, black, towering hemlocks. But maybe that was part of it. The trees themselves were also a tower.

I could cut the trees down, she thought. If I need to, I will cut the trees down.

She wondered why she would need to. She had finished her commitment to the vampire. It was over between them. It was just that she had a complaint to register. She said, "I didn't think Celeste would be *that* tired."

The vampire shrugged. The trees lifted and fell with his shoulders, swishing blackly. "I didn't promise degrees of tiredness," said the vampire.

Althea wet her lips, and the vampire, laughing, wet his lips.

She put a hand over her heart, and the vampire, laughing, put a hand over his heart.

He said, "All the gestures are blood symbols, did you realize that?"

"But you don't deal in symbols," she said.

"No."

Once more, the air thickened around them. The blackness of earth and sky faded to a predawn gray, and the gray was so thick that Althea thought she would suffocate, that the human body could not absorb clouds of wool. She panted, struggling for air, and stumbled away from the hemlocks toward the house.

The sun rose.

The tower of the house cast the first shadow of day. A shutter flapped where it had come unfastened. It sounded like a soul unhinged.

* * *

The school had its own broadcast studio.

The first week she attended high school, Althea had been awestruck. If you were the president of a club, or the captain of a team, you went on television and announced your meetings and games. What would it feel like to choose your outfit in the morning, knowing that you would be on television?

Kimmie-Jo had not been captain of Varsity Cheerleading when Althea was a freshman; a senior named Katya had held that honor. Katya was tall and lean and looked like an Ethiopian princess. She always wore the most awesome jewelry, and when she was on TV, Althea was overcome with admiration and amazement.

This year Kimmie-Jo made the cheerleaders' announcements. Her approach was markedly different. No exotic Cleopatra on the Nile, Kimmie-Jo was a bubblehead whose statements of when the game was, or where the practice was, or when Spirit Day would be, always sounded breathless and questioning, as if Kimmie-Jo was not entirely sure and was hoping a really kind football captain would help her out. Really kind football captains always did.

TV announcements were a time in which to say terrible things about people's hair or clothing or degree of nervousness. "It's Kimmie-Jo again! Does that girl bring her own hairdresser to school?"

"Oh, wow, look at that outfit. Kimmie-Jo could be one of those TV lifestyle reporters right now, in those same clothes."

"That would be a good career for Kimmie-Jo. Clapping and squealing. I think she has that down pretty well."

Althea never made cruel comments. If she were on the school TV, she would probably hide behind the principal rather than face the camera. She was filled with admiration for kids with nerve enough to appear live on TV. She dreamed of being the kind of girl who didn't even bother with notes, but chatted away, perfectly relaxed, as if having fun.

This afternoon, Mrs. Roundman came on. She was nicely named. Small, slightly chubby, pink-cheeked, relentlessly energetic. Althea felt that the young Mrs. Santa Claus had probably looked like that, pre-white hair and elves, so to speak.

"Good afternoon." Mrs. Roundman's smile vanished quickly, and she became fierce. "We have an unexpected vacancy on Varsity Cheerleading. Tryouts will be limited to those girls who tried out in September. Any girl who wishes to try out must commit four afternoons a week, plus the game schedule. She must have a C average or better. All girls planning to try out, sign up after school. Any girl who cannot come at the appointed hour, see me today with an appropriate excuse." Mrs. Roundman would never believe an excuse. If you were too busy to try out when Mrs. Roundman wanted tryouts held, you were worthless.

Althea's class burst into talk. "Who quit the squad?" they cried.

"Who got kicked off, more likely," said somebody.

"Who was it?" they demanded of Becky.

"Celeste," said Becky. "Isn't that weird? She telephoned Mrs. Roundman and said she just didn't have the energy for the season after all. She said it was taking too much out of her."

The boys looked doubtful that cheerleading could take that much out of you.

The girls looked doubtful that Celeste had ever wanted to be on the squad anyway, and it was her own dumb fault if she ran out of energy.

Althea tried to look ignorant of what had actually taken a lot out of Celeste. I must look sorrowful and concerned, she thought as she rejoiced.

Becky leaned toward Althea, her dark floppy ponytail quivering. "You should try out," said Becky to Althea. "You almost made it before, you know."

Even though she was thrilled at the compliment and the suggestion, Althea was a little bit shocked. Shouldn't Becky show more concern for Celeste? Hadn't they been friends? Shared practices and snacks all fall? Althea said uneasily, "Did you talk to Celeste? Maybe she'll change her mind."

Becky shrugged. "She's a quitter. Who needs a quitter? It's not that kind of squad."

The class echoed Becky. "She's a quitter. Who needs a quitter?"

But she had not quit, not really. She had been removed.

Becky said, "I'll coach you, Althea. You'll be perfect! You're exactly my height and figure, too, and

Mrs. Roundman is aiming for a better lineup. For example, although Amy's really good, Mrs. Roundman isn't going to take Amy, because Amy's too short. And she won't take Brooke, because Brooke has to be seven feet tall if she's an inch."

Althea cringed. Brooke was sitting right behind them. But of course Becky, being popular, had not bothered to look around first, because she didn't have to worry about people's feelings. They had to worry about their own.

"I'm five-eleven," said Brooke irritably. "And I'm not trying out, anyway. I have a full schedule. I'm much too busy to interrupt it for something as boring as cheerleading."

Becky and Brooke exchanged several more insults.

Then Brooke turned to Althea and smiled generously. "Good luck," she said. "You won't need it, though. You were so good at tryouts. I couldn't figure out why you didn't make it."

The smile caught Althea by surprise. It was so friendly. So honest. Maybe I will have friends who are not in cheerleading as well as friends on the squad, she thought. Maybe my life will be packed, like Brooke's. Althea smiled tentatively back at Brooke.

Becky and Althea walked down the halls, past the lockers, through the narrow passage to the coaches' offices, and into the girls' gym. Only one bleacher had been pulled out, and on that narrow bleached-gold bench sat — so few girls!

Althea couldn't get over it. Hardly anybody was trying out. *Perhaps,* the vampire had said, *I could arrange for the competition to be missing.*

"Wow," said Becky, "how come nobody's here, Mrs. Roundman?"

"Midseason replacements are problematic," said Mrs. Roundman. "The kind of girl we want is not a girl who sits around with an empty schedule. By now, such a girl has other commitments. She's a busy, active, involved person, or we wouldn't want her on our squad, anyway."

"I don't have other commitments," said Althea nervously.

Mrs. Roundman hugged her. "I think you knew a spot would open up, Althea," said the coach. "Your commitment to cheering is very strong. I can absolutely feel it, Althea!"

Mrs. Roundman took them through grueling warm-ups. Then she led them outdoors, into the same courtyard as before.

The sun was not so strong. A slight chill rose up from the grass. Althea swallowed. Becky shouted advice. Mrs. Roundman shouted orders.

A dozen kids gathered around to watch.

One of them was Celeste.

Althea tripped and steadied herself on the brick wall. The brick was slightly warm, as if it were slightly human. Like Celeste, who seemed only slightly warm and slightly human.

Celeste's face was caved in, like a sleeping child's. She did not really cry. She just stared, her mouth sagging, as if she could not understand what was happening.

"Celeste, I told you to see the school nurse," said Mrs. Roundman sharply. "What are you doing here?"

Celeste mumbled something.

She doesn't even have the strength to move her lips, thought Althea.

Mrs. Roundman said, "Celeste, you are upsetting everybody. That's very thoughtless of you. You've surrendered your place on the squad, which in my opinion was the action of a quitter. So quit. Go. Leave. Now."

Nobody went to help Celeste. Nobody spoke up on her behalf. Nobody leaned down to carry the bookbag for her. Celeste could not hoist it from the ground and instead dragged it over the pavement by a shoulder strap. Only Althea watched her go. Everybody else had better things to do.

I knew he would give me popularity, thought Althea. But I didn't know he would give me Celeste's! I didn't know she had to lose everything for me to have something! I thought — I thought —

Far across the field, the football team was practicing.

Ryan and Michael were there. Ryan, who made sure Althea was going to McDonald's. Michael, who was so perfect.

Her heart pounded fiercely, nervously, desperately. I have to get on the squad. It's my ticket to Ryan and Michael. To Becky and parties!

Out of the sun, in a cold corner, stood eight girls in Junior Varsity cheerleading uniforms. Sullenly, they watched Althea and her competition. When Mrs. Roundman allowed a brief rest for a sip of water, the JV captain walked over. Her voice was hostile. "I don't understand, Mrs. Roundman," said the JV captain. "Why didn't you bump one of us up to fill Celeste's position? It's not fair to put a beginner on Varsity when you have eight trained, seasoned JV cheerleaders available."

Mrs. Roundman frowned slightly. She looked out over the grass, and the grass trembled slightly, as if invisible feet were passing by.

"You don't have a reason, do you?" said the JV captain, trembling with anger. "You just felt like bypassing the JV squad."

Whose feet had just passed by? Who had persuaded Mrs. Roundman? What was out there on the grass?

Mrs. Roundman said, "You people are having such a fine season, with your own great coach, that I was hesitant to make any such change. There will be more squad changes when football season is over."

The JV captain brightened. "This is a temporary addition, then? Until basketball season? There'll be new tryouts then?"

"We'll see how everything works out," said Mrs. Roundman, and the JV squad went away less hostile.

Althea did not like that word *temporary*. Nor that phrase "We'll see."

Football season was half over, anyhow.

Is my popularity already half over, too? thought Althea. Is this all I get? A taste? A few weeks?

Chapter 7

But the days to come were sunny and golden.

Everything seemed bright, as if the world were made of daffodils and lilies, of springtime and sweet breezes.

How warmly the rest of the squad greeted her! Kimmie-Jo gave a charming little speech about how Althea was absolutely perfect for the team. Becky gave a little speech about how she and Althea were becoming great, great friends, and Becky knew that Althea would be a great, great friend to the whole squad.

Mrs. Roundman took pains to fit Althea's uniform perfectly. On the snowy white sweater the golden initials flared like a sunburst.

"Although Celeste was a lovely girl," said Mrs. Roundman, smoothing Althea's thick gleaming hair where the pullover had mussed it up, "with that pale coloring she simply did not shine the way you will, Althea."

Over the next several days she worked very

hard. Becky and Mrs. Roundman stayed after regular practice to help with the tougher routines. Saturday afternoon would be her first public performance, her first football game.

But either the girls were kind, or she really was good enough. Nobody yelled at her. Nobody made a face when she needed a second or third try, though once was enough for the rest. Nobody said they wished Celeste were still around.

After the hardest, longest afternoon of her life — Friday before the game — Althea staggered back to the locker room. She took a shower there, instead of waiting till she got home, something she would normally never have done. There is nothing worse than a girls' gang shower. Except maybe leaving the locker room with three hours of sweat clinging to your body.

She toweled off, blowing her hair dry, putting her earrings back on (Mrs. Roundman seemed to be morally opposed to anything that dangled), and fixing the collar beneath her pullover sweater just the way she liked it. Exhausted, she made her way to the front hall.

The high school foyer was a handsome space, with black marble floors and gray-striped marble walls. Announcements, bulletins, and the Artwork of the Week were taped everywhere. Scattered on the plant ledges and the steps were kids waiting for rides or the phone.

One was Celeste. She looked like a plant herself, drooping and in need of water. She was wearing an old dress, with too much material for her skinny body, and she was tucked into a corner of ledge and wall as if she needed several props because her bones had given way. Nobody sat with her.

Althea turned her back. It was best to accept things. Celeste had gotten too much too soon, and she would have to scrape her life back together and that was that. Althea could not get involved. Althea had enough pressure right now, what with her first game the next day.

Althea raised her chin, flipped her hair, and thought cheerleader thoughts.

Footsteps approached her. A voice said her name.

Althea cringed. She could not make herself turn around. I can't talk to Celeste, she thought, I absolutely can't, it's too much to ask. Why didn't she quit school as well as quit the squad? It isn't fair of her to keep showing up and making me remember —

A hand touched her. A hand that felt like a sponge, that seemed to have no bones and no blood.

Althea tried to run but she was rooted to the spot. She turned her head, and only her head — and it was Jennie Marsden.

Jennie had been Althea's closest friend before high school. Jennie had been the one to telephone, to sleep over, to giggle and gossip with. What friends they had been! That inseparable, essential intimacy of junior high friendship — when sleep is not possible until you share every single one of the day's thoughts on the phone.

But almost the first day of freshman year, Jennie found a whole new set of friends. She and Althea had hardly spoken since then, and when they did, Jennie was embarrassed and Althea was miserable.

"Jennie!" said Althea, relief sweeping through her with the velocity of race cars taking a turn. "Hi. Been a long time. How are you?" Althea's uniform, folded so the yellow letters could be seen and understood, lay on top of her notebooks. Swinging in her free hand were her blind-your-eyes-yellow pom-poms.

Jennie's eyes had landed on the precious sweater and the beautiful yellow letters. "You made Varsity!" said Jennie. "That is so great. I'm so happy for you!"

"Thanks," said Althea. I'm free, she thought. No more pain because Jennie got sick of me. I'm Althea, Varsity Cheerleader, and she's just Jennie, Former Friend.

"Yellow is your color," added Jennie. "It's your dark hair, I guess, and your fair skin. You look perfect."

"Thanks. I'm really excited about being on the squad."

"I'll bet," said Jennie enviously. "I never even dreamed of trying out. I could never do the routines. But you kept up your dancing and gymnastics, didn't you?"

Dancing and gymnastics we used to take together, thought Althea, and in her memory saw two little girls in matching leotards, tumbling, running around. Best friends.

Friend is a nice word, thought Althea. But *best friend* — that's beautiful.

She wondered dreamily who among all her new friends would become her best friend.

Althea made a quick and frightening decision. Becky had wanted her to have a party. She would schedule it right now, before she lost her nerve. Before she was overcome with hostess agony. "I'm having a party Sunday," she said. "Would you like to come? You'd like the rest of the cheerleaders, I'm sure."

Oh, how she loved saying that! The revenge of it! "Letting" Jennie come to a party.

"That would be so nice!" cried Jennie breathlessly. "It's so nice of you to think of me, Althea!"

Althea smiled generously. She walked carefully to the exit, keeping her eyes on Jennie, making herself forget that Celeste was on the far side of the foyer. Celeste, the only cheerleader who would not get an invitation. The only cheerleader who had been to the house before. The only one who knew.

"I love a party," said Jennie eagerly. "Want me to help?"

Althea's heart sang. Her feet danced. I'm having a party, and everybody will want to come! I did it. I'm popular! I have everything!

Chapter 8

The phone that had been so quiet for so long was busy every single minute.

Becky was delighted. "Of course I'll be there," she said impatiently, as if she and Althea had shared dozens of social events. "Call Kimmie-Jo," ordered Becky, "and have her call the rest of the squad."

"Is that polite?"

"It's the way it's done," said Becky. So Althea called Kimmie-Jo, who clapped her hands, a more frequent activity for Kimmie-Jo than for most, and said she couldn't wait and would call the others.

Althea telephoned Ryan, Scottie, and Michael. She, who had never had the courage even to look steadily into a boy's eyes, called ten boys. Everyone was delighted. Everyone said yes.

Partly it was because nobody had anything else to do on Sunday. She recognized that. Partly it was because they had never seen her house before, and it was the kind of house that everybody always wants to explore.

But partly, she thought, it's me!

With the last call completed, Althea walked slowly around the house, thinking of what she would have to do between now and then. Cleaning, shopping, food, music. The party must be perfect. It would be too cold out to dance on the porches or the lawn. Althea experimented with the furniture in the large parlor, moving it to this side or that to free up floor space.

"I'm considering," said the vampire, "who I want."

Althea's fingers closed spasmodically around the arms of a chair she had just shifted.

Where was he? How had he gotten in? From her crouching position she jerked her head back and forth to locate him. He was in the doorway, hands gripping each side. His fingernails were longer, and sharper, and seemed to be leaving dents in the woodwork. He rocked back and forth, chuckling to himself.

"So many choices!" said the vampire. The texture of his voice, usually dark, like pouring syrup, was much sunnier, as light and warm as honey.

Althea stood up. *So many choices.* He means my guests . . . he means . . .

No! This is my party! My first party! I'm popular now! He can't come back into this!

I could bash him to pieces with this chair, Althea thought. She picked it up.

"A chair?" said the vampire disdainfully. "I've avoided destruction for centuries now. A teenage girl with a chair is hardly going to slow me down."

Althea made herself set the chair down neatly and quietly to show that she was in complete control. "I'm just changing the furniture around," she said haughtily. "I am having a party this weekend, and you are *not* to be here."

His eyebrows rose. They arched like cathedral doorways, thin and pointed, vanishing under his straight black hair. With his eyebrows up, his eyes were very wide, too wide, as if they were glass balls that could fall out. "I'm quite looking forward to your party," he said. He let go of the doorway and admired his fingernails.

She thought of the people she had invited. Of the necks he could grip in those fingers.

"Get out," she whispered.

"My dear," he said.

How she hated the affection in his voice. As if they were companions of some sort! As if they had anything to do with each other! "I'm not your dear," she said. "Get out of my house."

"You forget, Althea, that I *come* with the house. I have been here longer than you, and I will be here long after you have departed."

Being addressed by name was far worse than being called "my dear." It was so much more intimate. It gave the vampire some sort of ownership over her. She wet her lips and tried to breathe evenly, but it was impossible; her lips stayed dry and her chest rose and fell like a panting dog's. "Go away," she said.

"I think not. Because I do have ownership over you, Althea."

He could read her mind? He was up inside her thoughts? Underneath her skull? Was nothing safe from him? Not heart, not veins, not even thoughts?

Althea felt the terrible cold of his presence, the wet woolliness of the air around him. "I gave you Celeste!" Her voice cracked.

"And so quickly, too," he agreed. "So craftily, carefully executed. I was grateful. But a party! Twenty guests! I am really quite eager to meet them."

She threw the chair at him.

But of course by the time the chair had crossed the room, he was elsewhere. "Try to control yourself," he warned. "There is nothing to be gained by childish impulses. You and I have been very adult with each other. We made a bargain."

"I kept it. I gave you Celeste. That's it. That's all it was, that's all it will ever be."

The vampire shook his head. She had seen him nod, many times; nod his head, nod his body, nod his cape. But she had never seen him shake his head no, and this, too, he did with his entire body, so that he rotated left, and then rotated right. She felt that he could bore a hole through the floor this way and drill himself into the cellar.

"That's not all it will ever be. There's always more. One is never satisfied with what one has, you see."

"I am satisfied! You come to my party, and I'll kill you! I will not have anything going wrong at my party! This is the first time any of them have ever been here. It has to be perfect."

"I'm afraid," said the vampire, his voice like spilled chocolate sauce, dark and spreading and impossible to clean up, "I'm afraid that you are incorrect, Althea. You cannot kill me. But in any event, nothing will go wrong at your party. It will be a wonderful party, my dear. You are a born hostess." He studied his horrid fingernails again, as if the wrinkled foil needed a touch-up. She envisioned him in some world, some room alien to her own, in front of some evil mirror, inspecting himself, admiring himself. He said, "The tower room, of course, will be left open. My dark path will intersect with —"

"No! There is to be no dark path anywhere! You don't get any more chances!" shouted Althea. "You had Celeste. That was your chance! So go away!"

"Althea, I hardly think that Celeste, and Celeste alone, is payment for what I have done for you. Cast your short little memory back over the last week. Ryan? Michael? Becky? Kimmie-Jo? Jennie?"

A terrible heat rose up in Althea, staining her cheeks red.

The vampire was amused. "Did you actually think they were paying attention to you because of the pull of your fine personality?"

Her heart turned into a furnace of rage and pain.

"How charming you look with those bloodred cheeks," said the vampire. "Blushing is a trait that's always appealed to me."

"You are sick," said Althea with loathing. Her whole body was trembling. Her skin literally crawled, as if it were coming off.

"No, Althea, I am not sick. I am a vampire. *You* made a choice, Althea. *You.*" He smiled at her, and the crescent of evil sparkled like diamonds, like the lost sparkle of Celeste's life. "You," he repeated, "you, you, you, you."

"That's true," said Althea. "But I'm not doing it again. I'm popular now, and that's what I wanted, and that's where we stop." She felt as if each muscle had detached from its bone and tendon and was fibrillating like a bad heart. How could he do this to her?

"Here's how we shall solve the problem," said the vampire.

"We shall solve it," said Althea in her hardest voice, "by you going away. Forever and ever and ever."

He tilted his head. He rested his crinkled-foil fingernails against his mushroom-colored cheek. He stroked his long earlobe. She had not noticed before how long his earlobes were. As if his victims, in the last struggle, tried to pull him off and stretched him. Very softly the vampire whispered, "And do you wish your popularity to go away, Althea? Forever? And ever? And ever?"

The shaking muscles grew still.

The pounding heart slowed.

The flushed skin went pale.

If he chose, the party that had not yet been would never be.

Nobody accepted my party invitation because of a slow day, thought Althea, or because they want to see the house, or get to know me better. The vampire made them accept. It's *his* party.

"You choose," the vampire said.

It was hard to talk or think or even exist. "Choose what?"

"Who crosses my dark path, of course. There will be twenty people you have invited, and no doubt twenty more you did not. You choose." He smiled.

She shook her head. "No. They're my guests."

"I'm your guest, too. You opened my shutters, did you not?" His voice was like tissue paper, floating slowly to the ground.

Althea decided to call his bluff. "You are depraved. You are demented. I will not do anything more that you ask. Accept that. I'm not giving in. Period. That's final," she added.

He smiled and nodded, his trunk pulsing back

and forth, as if feeling a pulse. Somebody else's pulse. Teeth hung over his narrow lips like foam on a sea wave.

"What is final," said the vampire gently, "is your popularity. Do you wish to make a fool of yourself at your first game? Do you wish people to laugh at you in public? Do you wish the squad to request Mrs. Roundman to remove you? Do you wish her, at halftime, to put in one of those oh-so-eager Junior Varsity cheerleaders instead of you?" His voice was slippery as silk and cruel as boredom. He said, "I made you. I will unmake you."

She thought, I can pretend to go along with him. That will give me Saturday's game and Sunday's party. Then I'll be safer, and I'll make it clear to him that this is over.

She turned the CD player on. Loud pulsing music, guitars and drums and keyboard, thrust its way into the room. It hammered and screamed, demanding attention. The vampire frowned and turned away. "Too loud for me," he said angrily.

She made a note of that. She would have the house shaking with noise.

"I wish to have one of your guests," said the vampire. His smile was no longer evil; it was sweet and innocent, like a child going to a picnic. "You choose the guest," said the vampire. "It's entirely up to you, Althea. I would not dream of taking a friend of yours. Surely there is somebody coming who doesn't matter. If not, simply invite a girl who doesn't matter. Lots of people don't matter."

I didn't matter a week ago, thought Althea. But I matter now. Am I going to give that up?

"At the party," he said, "make your choice clear by putting your arm around the shoulder of your choice. Then turn your choice to face those hemlocks that the sun goes down behind every night. When I see upon whose shoulder your arm rests, I will know who follows Celeste."

She picked up the chair and hurled it at him. An arm snapped off the chair, but the arms of the vampire were unharmed. She threw the chair again and again, until it was nothing but splinters.

The vampire was long gone.

Chapter 9

The tower was a black cone in a velvet sky. Black needle-tips of swaying hemlocks surrounded the tower like evil lace. Shutters banged with an oddly eager rhythm, as if something inside hoped to get out.

But no one heard.

Music screamed from every corner of the house, and the throbbing drum was the only beat the party guests heard.

The house was overflowing with teenagers.

Cars were parked everywhere.

In spite of the cold and the dark, a sizable group danced on the wide, pillared porch that circled most of the house. Some wore coats, some shivered in shirts. Several wrapped themselves and a chosen friend in a blanket and danced double.

In the kitchen, liters of soda were emptied so quickly they hardly seemed to have been swallowed — just absorbed into the party atmosphere.

In the living room, kids sat on the floor watching a DVD Becky had brought. In the family room, they lay on their backs on the rug, giggling hysterically at the jokes from a radio talk show Ryan had taped. On the stairs, kids sat in layers, like children playing school, moving up one or down one, laughing and talking about life and football victories. In the side yard, three members of the football team replayed especially precious moments of yesterday's game.

And what a game it had been! All the requirements of football had been met: It had been a beautiful day, blue-skied and chilly. The stands were packed. Beyond the stadium, autumn leaves were orange and red. The cheerleaders were brilliant, their uniforms as gaudy as circuses. The team was superb, their routines executed perfectly, their kicks as high as the goalposts.

And they won, of course.

It's true, thought Althea. Winning is everything. And I am among the winners.

It seemed to Althea that the house had been waiting for this evening. That, at last, the house could cast off doom and dark and return to the laughter for which it had surely been built. Its wide halls were meant for hand-holding couples, not ancestral portraits gathering dust. Its echoing parlor was meant for doubling the volume of music. Its huge kitchen was designed to feed dozens.

Althea circulated. She laughed here, chatted there, joined this group, and brought more chips and dip to that group. She sat briefly on the stairs finding an empty step just below Ryan, who gave her a backrub. It started off masculine and athletic, as if repairing muscles, and became softer, smoother, the harsh digs becoming affectionate strokes. She leaned back against him and held his hand in hers. He cupped her chin, tilted her head back, and they regarded each other upside down.

The house vibrated with music. Each area seemed to have been assigned to a particular sort of music: a hip-hop room, a dance-rock room, even a "Memories of Elvis" room. Everybody turned all this music up good and loud, and here in the stairwell it came together in one great chaotic throb. Speech was impossible.

The night before at Michael's had been wonderful. No kisses, but lots of friendly flirting. No best friends, but lots of loving laughter.

Being popular was temperature raising. Her cheeks glowed, her heart was full. She was hot with victory and joy. She was hoarse from cheering.

Ryan bent close over her cheek, and she held her breath, waiting for his kiss. But instead, he shouted in her ear, "I went upstairs. I hope you don't mind. I wanted to look into the tower room."

The tower room. A draft swirled down the long stairway and settled at the back of Althea's neck.

She had forgotten the vampire. Saturday — the game — the cheering — the victory — the party at Michael's afterward! There had been no room for thoughts of vampires. She had been all-teenager, all-high-school, all-pretty girl.

Ryan wanted to look in the tower room.

What shall I do? she thought. How can I stop this? Where is the vampire?

What if he appeared in front of people? What if they saw him?

"It's locked," said Ryan pleadingly. "I can't get in."

Althea smiled at him helplessly, as if locks on attic doors were the natural order of things and she could no more solve that problem than she could change the constellations in the sky. She pretended that the din of rock music made hearing and speaking impossible.

Ryan made sign-language gestures, and they went into the kitchen for something to drink.

How bright it was in there! The big double-wide fridge was open, with heads of two guests crammed in, inspecting the contents. On the counter perched a girl Althea didn't even know, crunching ice and eating potato chips. Somebody crashed my party, she thought, and she was oddly thrilled. You knew you were somebody when outsiders poured in, wanting to be part of the action.

I'm the action, Althea thought, and when Ryan spoke to her, she grinned widely and sparkled and giggled.

Ryan was only slightly taller than Althea, but much, much broader. He was wearing many layers: white cotton turtleneck under a dark blue fleece vest, with a darker leather jacket. It was a good choice; a little sober, perhaps, but oh!, so appealing. Thick as football armor, thought Althea. What would Ryan do if I hugged him? He'd probably hug back. It's that kind of party. But I've never hugged a boy. Do I start now? In my kitchen? With all these witnesses?

"You're hoarse," said Ryan worriedly. "Here. Have orange juice. Pack in that vitamin C." He pushed away the two heads at the fridge as if breaking up a huddle on the field, and one of the heads that popped up was Jennie's.

"Althea's voice is always hoarse like that," said Jennie, smiling at the memories of their shared childhood.

Ryan was disbelieving. "Come on. That's from too much cheerleading."

"You can never cheer too much," said Kimmie-Jo, taking her second Coke.

Jennie embarked on a long story of how she and Althea had once decided to be the jelly-doughnut-eating champions of the world. "It was sixth grade," said Jennie fondly, "and every single Saturday night we slept over at your house or mine, Althea. Remember? We began on jelly doughnuts on a Sunday morning. By Sunday afternoon . . ."

Althea had not thought of those sleepovers at Jennie's in a long time. What fun they had had, just the two of them!

"We had the nicest times, didn't we, Althea?" said Jennie softly.

Althea was filled with remembrance. They *had* had the nicest times. Althea's eyes grew teary. "Oh, Jennie, I've missed you!"

The girls moved toward each other, tentatively at first, and then springing across the kitchen. Althea even forgot Ryan. She thought only of that special friendship, the lovely silly years when life was golden, and doughnuts were good.

"I've missed you, too!" cried Jennie. "I don't know what happened when we hit high school. Something came between us! Let's not ever let that happen again!"

"Never!" cried Althea, full of friendship, full of love. She put her arm around Jennie's shoulder and hugged her tight.

Beyond the kitchen window, between the hemlocks, a path like a black sidewalk grew over the grass, slid across the porch, and crept through the silent windowpane. It left slime, gleaming like entrails.

Althea released Jennie and leaped back. "I didn't mean that!"

Jennie and Ryan stared at her.

Althea said, "I didn't hug you. You aren't my choice." Althea ran to the window to open it, screaming into the dark, "She isn't my choice."

But the window was already open.

The kitchen no longer smelled of potato chips and dip, of pizza and pepperoni. It smelled of mold and rot.

The kitchen was no longer bright and airy. The

atmosphere thickened. Ryan coughed and said he thought he'd go back to the other room. Jennie said dimly, "Althea?" Jennie's face was strangely blank, as if she had temporarily left her body. "I think I'll go outdoors for a while, Althea. I think I need fresh air."

"No," whispered Althea. "You don't need fresh air. Stay here, Jennie." I've got to hang on to her, thought Althea, keep her indoors. Keep her safe!

But she was too afraid. She hugged herself to keep from screaming again, and that left no hands free to reach out and hold Jennie.

Jennie's hand fumbled for the back door and could not find the knob. It did not matter. The knob turned by itself. Jennie stumbled forward and could not find the step. But it did not matter. A hand appeared to help her. A hand with long, warped fingernails. A hand the color of mushrooms.

Chapter 10

The debris of a finished party filled the house: crushed napkins and empty paper plates, ice melting at the bottom of glasses and pizza crusts on coffee tables.

"What a success it was," said the vampire. "You can be very pleased, Althea. And don't worry about the little scene in the kitchen. I will see that nobody remembers it."

Althea was screaming like a cheerleader, but throwing chairs and paintings and pieces of china instead of pom-poms.

"Jennie will not remember a thing," protested the vampire. "You saw Celeste. It takes energy to have a memory. Jennie's going to be very tired."

The smile that had stayed on Althea's face from Saturday's football game all the way through Sunday's party had exhausted her facial muscles. Now she had tics in both cheeks. Her face jumped and twitched. "That's not what I meant!" screamed

Althea. "I did not mean for you to touch Jennie! I yelled out the window. I told you to stop."

"Once things are set in motion," said the vampire, "they cannot necessarily be stopped."

"It was necessary!" she shrieked. "I told you to stop! Stopping was necessary!"

"I thought you said popularity was necessary," said the vampire. "You can't have both, you know. And you made your choice very clear."

"That's not what I meant when I hugged Jennie!"

"That's what you did, though," said the vampire. In the dark he glowed, like a phosphorescent fungus.

Althea ricocheted off the walls, pounding them, kicking them. "You know perfectly well that I was hugging Jennie because I felt affection for her!" screamed Althea.

"We agreed that when you put your arm around a girl at your party, it would be the girl who did not matter. In any event, there's no point in discussing it. It's done. It's over. There is no going back."

Althea's knees buckled. She tried to hang on to the wall, but the wall was flat and offered no support. She sank to the floor. The floor was filthy, where people had tracked in dirt and stepped on potato chips. "You — you — depraved — disgusting — horrible —" Althea could not think of enough words to fling at him. Jennie and I were going to be friends again! she thought. How dare he go ahead like that when he knew I didn't mean it!

"Kindly stop placing blame on others. It's *you,*" corrected the vampire. "I told you what the arrangement would be, and you accepted. *You* chose Jennie. *You* said this one doesn't matter."

Althea crushed a dreadful thought. That girl sitting on the counter, the one who crashed the party — why hadn't Althea put her arm around *that* girl? Nobody even knew her name! *That* girl didn't matter.

Althea's hands and heart and spine turned cold and stony. I thought that, she thought. I am a terrible person. I must not have that thought again. "Everybody matters," whispered Althea.

"Why didn't you feel that way with Celeste?" asked the vampire. He seemed calm, ready to talk philosophy all night if necessary. Not that there was much night left.

She had no answer.

"Because you wanted to be popular," the vampire told her. "It's very reasonable. We all want to be popular. You made a good choice, Althea. Why, everybody at your party wanted to come again."

She thought of the good-byes. So many hugs. She had been careful not to hug back, but nobody noticed. They said what a good time they'd had, what a neat house she had, what fun it was, how they must get together here all the time.

"What interesting people you had at this party," said the vampire. His voice was full of admiration.

It glowed, like a night-light in the hall. Safe and warm. "You have so many good friends now, Althea. Better friends than Jennie. How good a friend was she to you? Wasn't she mean? Didn't she abandon you? Didn't she leave you to sit alone in the cafeteria?"

It was true. Jennie had been rotten and nasty. And Althea did have better friends now. Nobody could put Jennie in the same class with cheerleaders like Becky. Jennie hardly mattered when you compared her to Becky.

Althea felt somewhat better.

"Think what a wonderful day Monday will be," said the vampire. He was leaving. She could see him growing down, dividing away, letting himself be absorbed into the thick woolly air around him. "Friends clamoring for your attention. Friends begging to come to the next party. Friends hoping to sit with you."

He was gone, and she was smiling. Friends. Oh, what a lovely, lovely word! She would have them like a bouquet of flowers in a bride's arms: all shapes and colors and sizes of them, all beautiful and happy to be there.

Friends.

Althea straightened and looked around the house. She began cleaning. The mess extended to every corner. She swept, she mopped, she neatened. Plenty of friends had volunteered to help clean up, but she had turned everybody down. She didn't want her first party to end with scrubbing and stacking. No, her first party had to finish with laughter, and the honking of horns, and the hugging of friends.

Friends, thought Althea. Her sweeping slowed down. Her energy evaporated. Jennie had once been a friend. Celeste had thought it was the act of a new friend to offer a ride.

Althea dropped down, becoming carpet, becoming rug, flat and thin.

Jennie would be like Celeste. Vibrance gone. Energy evaporated. Jennie would trudge.

And it will be my fault, thought Althea. I did it to her. My best friend. "No," said Althea out loud, "I couldn't have done that. Not me." Her voice was all scratch and no sound, like the leftovers of a soul.

How would Althea ever sleep again, knowing what she had done?

She had destroyed Jennie, Jennie of childhood memories and childhood joy. This is how I repay her, thought Althea. I sell her to a vampire.

Althea had cleaned up to the bottom of the stairs. At the top of the stairs waited the locked entrance to the Shuttered Room.

All I have to do, thought Althea clearly, is shut the shutters. I have to close him back up. Bolt him back in.

I can't save Celeste and Jennie now. It's too late for them. But I can still stop *him*. I can prevent him from doing it again.

She lifted her chin. Took the first step up. She felt strong and full of resolution. She was the kind of woman who could conquer whole worlds.

The vampire said, from behind the door of the Shuttered Room, "Do you want the first party to be the last party?"

Althea held the broom tightly.

"Do you want to find out if Ryan will ask you on a real date? Do you want to know if Michael enjoyed himself tonight? Do you want to know if Michael was just accidentally everywhere that you were? Do you wonder why it is that Michael did not bring along the beautiful, perfect Constance?"

Althea trembled. The broom fell from her fingers and tipped against the wall.

The vampire's voice was soft as cookie dough. "Do you want to see if Kimmie-Jo and Dusty will invite you to their parties? If Becky will?"

Althea slid to the bottom step and folded over on herself, like an old sheet in a musty linen closet.

"Of course you do," he whispered. The vampire's laugh was like old leaves on dying trees. "Now, get a good night's rest, Althea. What's done is done. And nothing has happened, really. Jennie's just going to be a little tired. And you have better friends than that now, anyhow, don't you?"

Chapter 11

Monday.

Althea had dreaded Mondays for a year and a half.

The terrible building into which she was forced to walk — alone.

That horrible cafeteria in which she was forced to sit — alone.

Each room so grim.

Whether the library or the gymnasium, the English class or the chemistry laboratory, each room seemed designed as a showcase for other people's friends.

Monday.

And Jennie would not be coming to school.

Althea considered being absent herself. Staying in bed all day. Or perhaps the rest of her life.

But in the end she got up, dressed, drove to school, and parked.

Every move was heavy as lead. Putting the parking brake on left her weak and panting. Pushing down the door locks was like bench pressing. How could she move herself across the pavement? She felt as heavy as the car itself, except that she had no wheels. She had to pick up each foot, and set it down, and then pick up the next one.

Althea trudged forward. Never had the walk seemed longer, the steps higher, the doors heavier.

But the door handle was taken from her, and a larger, stronger hand pulled it open for her. "Hi there," said a boy cheerfully. "How are you, Althea?"

She did not even recognize him. She did not even *know* him.

She murmured, "Thank you," and walked into the gleaming marble foyer.

"Hi, Althea!" called a girl changing the Artwork of the Week exhibit.

"Hey, Althea, you get that math homework?" yelled a voice.

She waved. She called. She answered. She even managed a smile or two. The entire school had learned her name. The power of Varsity Cheerleading! The publicity of standing in front of the entire school for two hours, yelling! These kids knew her; they felt loyalty and affection for her; they enjoyed seeing her cheer. She was theirs.

"Hi, Althea!"

"How are ya, Althea?"

"Sit with me, Althea."

Her name was used aloud more times that Monday than in all the years of her life.

Althea. The name rang in the cafeteria.

Althea. The name bounced off the gym walls.

Althea. The name was murmured in the library.

"Althea," as a name, had always seemed both odd and stodgy. Now it sounded beloved and welcome.

Fellow cheerleaders called to her; classmates wanted to chat with her; unknown kids going down the hall actually congratulated Althea on a good game Saturday, as if her cheering had brought about the victory.

Everyone who had been at the party came up grinning and delighted to say what fun it had been, how they hoped she would have another one soon.

And everyone who had not been at the party came up shyly and hopefully, hinting that Althea might include them next time.

But Jennie was absent.

Childhood memories filled Althea like those doughnuts: heavy and lasting. Jennie and Althea going to the petting zoo; Jennie and Althea playing Chutes and Ladders; Jennie and Althea buying spring hats and being too shy to wear them; Jennie and Althea taking riding lessons and being in horse shows together; Jennie and Althea drawing up lists of cute boys, back in elementary school when there was no such thing, and giggling insanely all night long at each other's houses, daring each other to phone a boy; Jennie and Althea cutting each other's hair so badly one sleepover that

Jennie's mother escorted them to a mall hairdresser who was open evenings.

Jennie was absent.

Althea found herself behaving vaguely to all who spoke her name. Don't be rude, she said to herself, pay attention! People are talking to you.

But curiously enough, her distracted manner made her more desirable.

She pondered this. The popular person who doesn't have time for you becomes *more* popular! she thought.

She saved up the faces of all who spoke and laughed, thinking — did I earn this? Or did the vampire somehow migrate to each of them, and instruct them in their sleep: *Admire Althea today.*

And tomorrow? Next month? Next year?

Will they forget me as quickly as weather? Will I vanish like last Monday's sunshine, or yesterday's snow flurry?

Jennie was absent.

Her mind returned continually to that.

The vampire will ask me for another one, she thought. Not right away. But soon.

Althea changed classes, ate lunch, went to the library, got books from her locker, and wondered who it would be.

Who?

Who will I give him?

Who will he take?

Like owls fluttering through the halls, their

wings hitting her hair, the cry *who? who? who? who? who?* rang in her ears.

I cannot do that again, she said to herself. I cannot destroy another human being! I can't participate in it anymore. That's all there is to it.

"You know, Althea," said Ryan's voice, "you're more daydreamy than I realized."

She jumped, astonished to find she was sitting in a chair, and that Ryan was sitting in a chair next to her. He was smiling into her eyes, his hand resting on the chair back. "Hi, Ryan," she said, blushing. His hand shifted from the back of the chair to the back of her neck.

His fingers were callused, but his touch was gentle. He touched her skin as if exploring new worlds, lightly tugged her hair, and watched what he was doing, fascinated by his skin against hers.

Althea swallowed, thinking of somebody else who liked the backs of necks. *Jennie is absent.*

She took Ryan's hand and held it in her lap instead. He was delighted and looked at their two hands together. He separated her fingers with his and intertwined them, making a row of ten knuckles: her smooth, small, pale knuckles alternating with his large, knobby, dark ones.

"The school day," he said, managing a laugh, "has ended. Did you notice? You want to go for a drive? Maybe pizza. I can always eat pizza. I could eat yours if you're not hungry."

Michael appeared beside them. "Holding hands in public?" he teased. "I'm shocked, Ryan."

"Get lost," said Ryan cheerfully. "We're going for pizza."

Ryan pulled Althea to her feet. The library was full of kids doing research papers or homework. All were watching. She felt their eyes. The cheerleader and the football players. The popular girl and the handsome boys. The one you dream of being.

And it's me, she thought. *It's me.*

Chapter 12

The three of them made their way out of the school, bumping into one another, laughing, pushing on the steps, sheltering one another against the wind. Althea, confused about why they were a threesome, said aloud, "Michael, are you coming, too?"

Michael and Ryan roared with laughter.

"It's my car he's inviting you to use," explained Michael. "Old Ryan here is without a vehicle. If you plan to see much of the guy, keep in mind that he's going to need a chauffeur from now on."

"What about the car with three broken doors?" said Althea, who yearned to slither and slide in and out with Ryan.

Ryan sighed heavily. "The police. The cops."

She was horrified. "You were arrested?"

Ryan looked hurt while Michael grinned. "I was not arrested," Ryan said with dignity. "The police pulled me over because they could not understand how I was able to get out of such dented doors. It seems that vehicle inspection standards require that the driver and passenger should be able to get out of the car. I argued that we *are* able to get out of the car — it just takes a little while. The police said, What if I had a passenger who wasn't that agile? I said, Well, I just wouldn't take him along, would I? The police said, What about in situations where we didn't have a while to take? Like breaking down on the train tracks. I pointed out that there are no train tracks. He didn't care. He said I can't drive a one-door car until I get it fixed."

"But he's not going to get it fixed," said Michael. "It would cost a fortune."

"So yesterday," said Ryan, "I buried my servant, the car."

"It's gone to that great junkyard in the sky," said Michael.

The boys stood reverently for a moment, hands on hearts, mourning the passage of a really good vehicle.

Althea laughed helplessly, adoring them both.

She had never been able to comprehend a girl who would dangle two boys. You would think the girl would choose the better boy, get rid of the crummier one, and settle into having a great time.

Now she could see this was not such a great course of action.

Here was Ryan: sweet and funny. Cute and built and bright.

Here was Michael: all of the above, but more so.

They traveled in a pair, obviously.

She had her own car; she could drive Ryan; they could dispense with Michael. But what girl in her right mind would dispense with Michael? On the other hand, what girl in her right mind would dispense with Ryan, either?

Ryan, Michael, and Althea drove around for a while, all three in the front seat. Althea was wonderfully crushed between their thighs, and when Michael took a sharp turn, his arm on the steering wheel brushed against her, and when Ryan leaned forward to talk to Michael, his shoulder pressed on hers.

Althea thought that probably nothing, including sex or being elected president, could be as splendid as sitting in the front seat, Michael and Ryan talking to her at the same time, their wonderful masculine presence and scent and attitudes filling her with utter contentment.

Eventually, they arrived at Pizza Hut.

Of course Pizza Hut is a perfectly public restaurant, open to the world, and Althea had been there many times. And yet, if you walked in and passed the salad bar and went to the rear of the restaurant, there was a booth in the corner that was virtually a private club.

The high school club.

It was occupied continuously by one group or another, its numbers changing, diminishing, increasing, as one popular person drifted away, only to be replaced by another.

Only six could actually fit in the booth.

Usually seven or eight were crammed in, while several more sat at right angles in the adjoining, non-corner booths, which lacked the special status of the crammed corner.

In her previous life, Althea would hardly have had the nerve to lift her eyes even to look toward this corner.

In her wildest dreams, in her most desperate prayers, she had never hoped to be escorted to it by Michael and Ryan.

They had hardly been seated, hardly begun to argue over whether the pizza should have peppers and pepperoni, when Kimmie-Jo and Dusty arrived.

How interesting popularity is, thought Althea. I am with Michael and Ryan, and that is perfection, and everybody is envious, but the real stamp of approval is from the girls. Kimmie-Jo and Dusty will decide it. Boys come and go, but girlfriends stay, and judge, and count.

Kimmie-Jo shrieked, "Hi, Althea, how's your throat?" and slid into the seat.

Dusty said, "Althea, thank goodness you're here. There's so much to talk about."

Althea laughed to herself, and when Ryan tugged her backward, so that she was leaning against his chest, she cooperated fully.

Becky came into Pizza Hut.

Althea was amazed to see Becky pause by the salad bar, unsure of herself. Becky's eyes quickly scanned the booths, to see where she would be welcome. Michael, Ryan, Althea, Kimmie-Jo, and Dusty were in the corner booth. A bunch of juniors had taken the booth on one side, and some seniors the opposite booth. Becky, like Althea, was a sophomore. A cheerleader, yes, but not old enough, and with too little status to break into the Kimmie-Jo/Dusty booth.

I've already moved ahead of Becky! thought Althea, seeing popularity suddenly as a sort of board game, where a throw of the dice, or somebody else's lost turn, had you whipping ahead, gathering points, heading for the winner's circle.

Althea waved to Becky, calling, "Come on over here, Becky, we have plenty of room."

Kimmie-Jo and Dusty frowned slightly. Becky came up breathlessly, her cheeks turning pink with excitement. Ryan and Michael acknowledged her politely.

Becky was really only a fringe member of the popular crowd. Only being on the Varsity Squad had moved her onto that fringe. Only during games and practices would she really count. Here, at Pizza Hut, Becky was minor.

Althea was overcome with a sense of power. She — who had been nobody! Nothing! Invisible! Inaudible! She could bestow popularity on Becky.

Ryan said to Althea, "So when's the next party? That one was so much fun."

Parties, thought Althea. She landed slightly, not all the way; part of her was still flying. But part of her was grounded. As Jennie had been. As

Celeste had been. She had made two choices. And now Jennie was absent; Celeste was trudging. And for what? For a slice of pizza eaten in this corner instead of that?

"I had a great time," agreed Michael.

"Me, too," said Becky quickly.

"I don't know how often I can open up the house like that," said Althea carefully.

"I know just what you mean," said Kimmie-Jo, although that seemed unlikely. "My parents get so anxiety-ridden when I even suggest a party that it's pathetic."

Talk turned to parental rules. Ryan quickly lost interest and stood up, handing money to the cashier. "Hey, Mike," he said, "you want to haul us back to the high school so we can get Althea's car?"

"Sure."

They got up. A trio. A successful popular trio. Althea was dizzy with it. "Bye, Kimmie-Jo," she said. "Bye, Dusty."

Becky shrank down into the booth. She was excess baggage now. Her hostess had left; the rulers of this booth had better people to associate with.

Althea cringed for her. "Becky?" said Althea quickly. "You want to sleep over one night this weekend? Saturday?"

"Hey," protested Ryan. "I'd like to sleep over one night this weekend."

Althea laughed, although her soul and body burned at the thought, and kept her eyes safely on Becky.

"I'd love to," said Becky, no longer shrinking. She sat tall and relaxed. Althea had spoken to her. Althea had included her.

No wonder the ancient Greeks portrayed the god Zeus with a lightning bolt. Althea could have held electric power lines and made them do her bidding. She was popular now, and the words looked and sounded alike:

Popular.

Powerful.

So Jennie was absent. So big deal. It was like any football game: You had some winners, and you had some losers.

Althea had become the winner.

Chapter 13

They had taken only one step into the parking lot — a trio of dancers getting one beat into the choreography — when a gleaming black SUV drove up. Several laughing girls rolled down their windows and called, "Hi, Michael. Hi, Ryan."

The girls were seniors — and one of them was Constance.

"Hi, Althea," the girls chorused.

Althea was awestruck. Her name was known to this set? Constance and her beautiful friends? "Hi," she whispered.

The black SUV rolled on, inch by inch; the driver had decided not to stop all the way, but to creep ever forward. Althea thought that was just right for the personality of this crowd: Nothing would stop them, and they would stop for nothing. They were the girls who would have it all.

Oh, to be one of them!

As the SUV glided past, Althea let a fantasy drift through her mind in which she mixed with this group, and laughed among them, and danced among them, and was the girl who had it all.

Ryan stepped back, pulling Althea with him, but Michael stood still, as if waiting to be run down.

Although the SUV slipped on, Constance opened the passenger door and leaned out a few inches. How lovely she was! Constance deserved to be the only model for an entire magazine. Softly, as if alone with him in a shadowy room, Constance said, "Michael. How are you? I miss you."

Michael flushed and said nothing. He seemed unprepared, like a child among adults. What had happened between these two, to make Michael stiff with nervousness and Constance soft with hope?

"May I join you?" said Constance, half out the door.

Michael smiled courteously, opened the door the rest of the way, and said, "Of course."

Now the SUV stopped.

Constance emerged. She was wearing a white wool skirt and a white silk blouse with full sleeves. A brilliant scarf lay carelessly around her throat. She looked the way every girl dreams of looking: beautiful, romantic, and mysterious.

Althea felt dumpy and dumb. No longer even felt sixteen — maybe eleven. A little kid stumbling behind a beauty queen.

The SUV moved on, circling Pizza Hut and vanishing. Michael got behind the wheel of his car with Constance beside him in the front. Althea and Ryan got in the back. It was an entirely different drive. There was no silly joking. Michael drove with great concentration, never looking at the passenger on his right. Constance sat sideways, stretching her safety belt out like a first-prize ribbon to be admired, and never took her eyes off Michael.

Constance was trying to make peace. Over what rift, Althea would have loved to know. Michael and Constance were extremely courteous to each other. Their dialogue might have been heard a hundred years ago, in more elegant times, perhaps over teacups and lace doilies. Althea was glad they had not had to talk over pizza.

She remembered Ryan and looked his way. Ryan was picking grumpily at some torn threads on his blue jeans. "Michael," he said, "you're just steering. You forgot about driving us back to get Althea's car."

Michael grinned in embarrassment. He said, "I thought I'd circumnavigate the globe. Skip high school."

"As long as you don't skip me anymore," said Constance.

For the first time Michael looked at his girlfriend and then rested his hand on her knee. She covered his hand with hers, and Althea sighed with contentment. True love had won.

Michael and Constance both laughed a little, and then were suddenly self-conscious in front of

Althea and Ryan. Constance smiled at the back-seat. "I don't know if Michael's ready to be alone with me," she said cheerfully. "I think we need you two in the backseat. So how are you enjoying Varsity, Althea? I was so glad you made the squad."

"I love it," said Althea shyly. "I'm making friends already. I didn't think I would make friends so quickly."

"We're writing essays on friendship for English," said Michael. "It's a tough subject. The first essay was what friendship *gives* to you. You had to be specific and name three friends who gave you something: one from elementary school, one from a sport or an activity, and one who's not your own age."

Althea's hands were so cold. She felt as if blood had stopped circulating through her. Perhaps it had. Perhaps that was how the vampire migrated. Perhaps the vampire could dictate what they talked about, perhaps he could give out English assignments.

What if I had to set down on paper what my last two friends gave me? she thought. They gave me popularity. Jennie's the friend from elementary school, and Celeste's the friend from a sport. They gave me this. They're the reason I'm sitting h 're, with Ryan putting his arm around my shoul er, Constance smiling at me, and Michael tall ng to me.

And that third category . . . a friend not y ur age. Could that be what the vampire wanted n xt?

"Now the second essay, which I have to write tonight," said Michael, "is what *you* give to others in a friendship."

What I gave, thought Althea, is unspeakable. Unwritable. Unthinkable. But I did it anyway. I did it twice.

Ryan's large smooth hand had encircled her now and was pulling her against him, so that she was snuggled into the curve of his arm. He tilted his head against hers, and the warmth of him, the masculine presence of him, oh, it was the most wonderful thing she had ever experienced.

I wouldn't change my mind, thought Althea. I wouldn't have done it differently.

I'm sick. I'm horrible. I'm the worst person on earth. Because I'm glad it happened. I'm glad I have this ride, and these new friends, and Ryan!

Constance was still facing Michael, drinking him in almost. Her lovely profile was outlined by the setting sun, and the perfection of her gave Althea shivers.

I want to be like that, she thought. I want to be just like Constance.

She thought: I just won't think about Celeste and Jennie anymore. That's the important thing. Not to dwell on it. I have what I have. The past is past.

"It's a tough essay question," said Michael, frowning slightly. "I mean, what *do* I give to my friends?" He sent Constance a look of deep meaning, and she returned it by lifting his hand and holding it against her cheek. Althea loved the privilege of being there to see it.

"Pizza and rides are all you give your friends," teased Ryan.

"I want to get an A on that essay, you jerk," said Michael. "It has to be profound. Think of something meaningful."

"There's nothing more profound than a really good pepperoni pizza," said Ryan.

"What do you think, Althea?" Constance asked. "If you wrote about friendship, what would you say?" Constance rested her chin on the seat back and looked straight into Althea's eyes.

Every hair on Althea's head prickled.

Constance fills the requirement. She is not my age. So she must be next.

Constance? Beautiful, wonderful, lovely Constance? Getting draggy and trudgy and pitiful like Celeste? Never! That must never happen! Althea forgot to censor her speech. Right out loud she said, "I guess you don't turn a friend over to a vampire."

Michael, Constance, and Ryan burst out laughing. Michael laughed so hard he almost drove off the road. Ryan hugged Althea more tightly, as if that were a cue line for a lover; as if that statement meant they understood each other now and were actually dating, a romantic pair.

"What a great rule," said Michael, shaking his head, and getting back into the proper lane. He turned on his headlights as the sky finished darkening and the winter night closed in. He turned on the heater, and a warm wind caressed Althea's ankles.

"Next time I meet a vampire," promised Constance, "I won't turn a single friend over to him."

Laughter filled the car, as if a new form of oxygen had been created, as if a different combination of elements had invaded their little enclosure.

Michael turned up Hillside Drive.

Far away and far below, the many-angled roof of Althea's forbidding house was like a black pool in the early darkness of winter. Three chimneys, solid brick, faded red, reached up toward the night sky.

And one tower.

With three windows.

Whose shutters banged.

Michael was driving so slowly that the world seemed to have slowed down with him. Even the wind seemed to lift the bare branches slowly, while autumn leaves fluttered to the grass slowly, and people getting out of their cars closed their doors slowly and walked slowly inside.

Althea seemed to watch the shutters of her tower for a long, long time; time enough for seasons to change and friendships to end.

They were dark green shutters, shutters the color of ancient hemlocks, the color of impenetrable forests.

He's waiting for me. He'll be there when I get back. He needs somebody else. He'll want Con-

stance. But I cannot, cannot, cannot do that! Michael and Constance are so perfect together. I love them together. I love knowing that there is such perfection in the world. Such beauty.

The shutters moved in unison toward the center of each of the three windows. Gently they closed themselves. One by one, they shut out the night.

Night . . .

There had been a conversation about night . . .

What had she agreed to do at night?

Althea's hair lifted from her scalp, as if the vampire were running his horrid fingers through it, his tarnished foil nails scraping her scalp. Her spine hurt.

I invited Becky to spend the night on Saturday, she thought. I forgot Becky. I forgot her as quickly and easily as I decided to forget Celeste and Jennie. It's as if I have already given Becky away. So that I can keep Constance.

Horror filled Althea like quicksand, pulling her down the hill, hauling her body by evil gravity toward the shutters.

Toward the vampire.

Toward the end of Becky.

Chapter 14

There was so much to be afraid of!

Herself, and her capacity to do evil things.

The vampire, and his presence, the way he was changing her.

The future, and what she chose.

The friends she had, and how she would hurt them. Or hurt herself.

And this: driving Ryan home. Alone with a boy in a car.

The dark of night was a capsule around them. The interior of the car was their world. How much less relaxed they were, without Michael and Constance to dilute their emotions. They had been a group: easy laughter, easy talk. Ryan's hand rested lightly on her shoulder as she drove, and his fingers for a moment touched her hair.

The touch spooked her, and she suppressed a shudder.

She could feel the vampire behind her, thinking of her, planning for her, waiting.

Up and over yet another hill she drove.

When she came down the other side, a mass of soil and rock blocked the vampire. It was impenetrable. His dark path could not go that far; she could feel in her ribs, her spine, the flesh of her back, that they had reached some kind of safety.

She knew, as firmly as she knew her numbers and her alphabet, that the vampire could not pierce the hill.

Althea heaved a great sigh of relief. It was so huge that Ryan jumped away from her, startled, jerking his hand back and staring at her.

"Sorry," she said lamely. "I — I guess I don't drive much after dark, and I — I guess I'm kind of tired. So I sighed."

Ryan found that a difficult excuse to accept. "It's okay," he said stiffly. "Just drop me off and go straight home. You probably have lots of homework anyway."

She had a sense that she was losing him, that he was fading away from her as fast as daylight had faded on this wintry afternoon. She caught his hand to yank him back. "No, no," she protested. "I'm just really not that much of a driver."

He believed her. How amazing. If some dumb girl said that to Althea, she certainly would have some questions. What American teen ever said or believed for a single moment that he or she was a lousy driver? Nobody. Everybody on earth believes they're an excellent driver. Everybody on earth takes pride in their brilliant driving skills.

But Ryan believed her.

Did the vampire make him? she thought. How much power does the vampire really have? Can he actually invade my friends' thoughts?

Of course he can. Or he wouldn't make them my friends.

A gruesome thought invaded Althea. Had the vampire been giving Ryan instructions? Touch her. Smile at her. Take her hand.

She had to ask the vampire next time she saw him; she had to know how much of this was real. Does it count if he makes it happen? she thought. What if I find out it's not for real? Will I still be thrilled to see Constance smile, and have Ryan hug me and Michael say my name?

Ryan lived in a ranch-style house. His driveway was paved, not gravel like hers. It seemed firmer, more modern, less likely to harbor things.

"Want to come in?" said Ryan.

"I'd love to another day," she said, "but I have to get home." She kissed him. She was absolutely astounded at herself. Where had that courage come from?

Ryan, startled and pleased, kissed her back.

They laughed and kissed a second time, breathless and surprised in their sharing. Althea drove away into the night, so full of joy that she felt nothing else could ever exist in her except gladness. She liked a boy, and a boy liked her. What else is there?

She laughed all the way back to her house.

The laugh stayed on her face, like an echo in the air. The curve of her smile kept her face alight and aloft.

She was still laughing when she came in her own door, and the vampire said, "I was out tonight. Did you feel me? Did you know I was there?"

He smiled, framed by the huge, carved doorway, and his smile increased to match the door. His mouth filled more of his face than usual. His teeth were long and sharp as garden stakes.

"Get out of here!" Althea hissed. Forget the questions she had wanted to ask him! She was furious with him for existing, for making her think about what she had done. How could she find peace of mind if she was forced to remember?

"I beg your pardon," said the vampire. "I live here."

"It's my house!" she shouted. She stamped her foot. The porch shook a little from the force of her pounding foot, but the vampire was not affected.

"It's mine," said the vampire, lingering on the sentence. Then softly, he echoed himself, drooling over the words, *"It's mine."*

Althea could not get in her own door. He filled it. His swirling black cape went right up to the edges of it, like pond scum.

"And you," said the vampire, smiling cruelly, "you are mine, also."

Chapter 15

She was doing her math homework when the phone rang. Page 78. Quadratic equations lined up like little vehicles trying to cross the page. The book was very white, and the numbers printed very clearly, very thinly, like a message.

"Hi, Althea?" said an eager girl's voice. "It's Becky."

"Hi, Becky!" cried Althea.

A girlfriend was phoning. It had been years! Years since the joy of having a best friend to call up and gossip with. Althea beamed into the telephone, as if it had been invented just for her.

"I had such a good time at Pizza Hut, didn't you?" said Becky.

"It was great, wasn't it? Isn't Michael funny? Isn't Ryan terrific?"

"Oh, yes, and afterward, after you left with the boys — well, I stayed on awhile and got to know Kimmie-Jo and Dusty so much better. Kimmie-Jo told me all about this terrific place where she gets her hair done. Dusty thinks I should maybe get mine a little more layered in the back. Dusty thinks I need more volume in my hair."

Althea loved to talk about hair. She told Becky that she, personally, thought Becky's hair was extremely attractive, the way it clung to her head, and Althea loved the ponytail, which was exactly the right length, shoulder length. Becky could curl her hair for elegant occasions, but if Becky cut it layered, she would have volume, but no ponytail. And was that really what Becky was after?

Becky said she was really after a boyfriend, and hair volume kind of ran second to that.

They laughed shrilly and eagerly into the phones, and got into more comfortable positions, because this was a conversation with all-night potential. Althea was sorry she had no snack next to the phone. Althea frowned at her quadratic equations and did one.

After they were done with hair, they moved on to makeup and clothing, and then they got to the important part: what Althea had done with Michael and Ryan. Althea told Becky everything, while Becky sighed in vicarious pleasure at each description. ". . . and then he took his hand off my shoulder and touched my hair," said Althea.

"How did he touch it?" Becky said. "I mean, did he run his hand over it, or through it, or what?"

Althea did another quadratic equation. A really good equation, thought Althea, is a girlfriend on the phone asking what you did with a boyfriend in the car.

They discussed exactly what happened, Becky moaning with envy. They pondered whether Althea, too, needed more volume in her hair and should go with Becky to the new hairstylist. Then Becky was struck by the thought that perhaps Dusty and Kimmie-Jo had been trying to say that Becky looked stupid and needed professional help.

"You know them better than I do," said Althea. "Are they mean or nice? Are they thoughtful or cruel?" Althea finished up two more equations.

Becky told several interesting stories about various nice or else cruel things that Kimmie-Jo and Dusty had done. Then she said casually, and yet carefully, ". . . about sleeping over, Althea? I asked my mother about Saturday. But I thought I should check first and see if, you know, if Ryan, like, asked you out. Because I mean, I wouldn't hold you to your invitation if Ryan — well — he would come first, of course."

Althea suddenly remembered why she had stopped being friends with Jennie when they hit high school. It had been a conversation just like this one. How could she possibly have forgotten? The pain had paralyzed Althea for months! For her whole freshman year.

The conversation replayed in Althea's head like an old record: one of those big, slow records that you found boxes of at yard sales, because nobody even owned a turntable anymore.

"But you said I could stay over at your house Saturday," Althea had protested.

"I know, Althea, but grow up! Dave asked me to the movies! I mean, what counts here, Althea?"

"I'm your best friend."

"Althea!" (How irritated Jennie had sounded; as if she were looking at her wristwatch; as if she could not believe her romance was being slowed down by this dumb, dumb, dumb conversation with some worthless girl.) "Althea, this is a boy. Remember how there are two sexes? Of course, you haven't found out yet. But I have. And I'm not about to tell Dave I can't go to the movies because my friend Althea wants to come over!"

That Saturday night seemed eons ago, but it wasn't. It was only a year and a half.

A year and a half ago that the best friend of all her life, and all her joys and sorrows, had said, "Let me spell this out for you, Althea. I have a boyfriend now."

Jennie had not added — had not needed to — *I don't want you, Althea. I'm not available now. I have better things to do. Better people to be with.*

Memory was harsh and painful.

I'm not that kind of friend, she thought, proud of herself. I wouldn't write a friend off into the background like that. She said firmly, "Of course it's on, Becky. I can hardly wait. There's only one trouble. Is there any chance that I could stay at your house instead of you at mine? I mean —

well — you know how it is — I just can't have company right now."

Becky replied delicately that she understood; families could be difficult. "I'd love to have you stay here," said Becky. "Actually, that's better in a way, because even though I'm sixteen, my parents don't like me to stay overnight at anybody's house when they haven't met the family. They're really old-fashioned, Althea, you wouldn't believe it. I have so much to tell you."

Althea folded up into her chair and cuddled the phone like an infant. She was safe for another weekend, at least. Nobody would be here to cross the dark path.

"Ryan didn't ask you out for Saturday, then?" Becky asked just to be sure.

"Even if he had, I would have explained to him that I had to check with you first. I'm not that kind of friend, Becky."

She could almost see Becky smile: that wide, delighted, pixieish smile that made her such a great cheerleader. That uptilted head, that crowing laugh, that low-volume hair, and twitching ponytail!

Althea giggled into the phone. Becky's giggle matched, and they agreed to meet before school in the morning, to talk about essential things before class began.

Althea hung up. She smiled, thinking of friendship. What a beautiful thing it was. She looked down regretfully at her next quadratic equation and lifted her pencil to finish off the homework.

An oddly clear shadow crossed page 78.

A shadow like glass or mirrors.

The vampire said, "I have decided. I want Becky next."

Chapter 16

Becky's ranch house was on a hillier and rockier lot than Ryan's. The driveway was cut deeply into the earth, with high stone sides that dripped with dank climbing ivy. Hemlocks planted many years ago had grown into monsters, shouldering their way toward the windows.

Becky went in through the garage, which was dark and tumbling with boxes and shadows, leading Althea into a lower-level rec room.

Dark brown carpet and dark-paneled walls made a mockery out of the word *recreation*. Althea could not imagine bouncing, cheerful Becky inhabiting such a grim cellar of a room. She could well imagine the vampire inhabiting it, however.

Becky bounded up another set of stairs to the kitchen/living room level.

Althea frowned. On the third step she turned and looked back. A shadow clear as glass drifted behind her.

Althea shut the rec room door firmly behind

her. It was a thin door, a weak and shallow door. A door that would stop nothing.

Upstairs, mercifully, was bright and light.

The kitchen was packed with broccoli-green cabinets. The living room had been decorated to look like a garden, with white wicker furniture, and fanciful flowers danced on the drapes and cushions.

Perhaps the dark and brown things of the world would stay downstairs, and the light and bright would control the upper level.

Becky flung open the door to her own bedroom. Althea had never seen so much purple, so many hues and shades of lavender, violet, amethyst, and mauve. "I love your room," she whispered. She soaked up the joy of the room, the sheer exuberance in life that Becky's room was.

"Me, too," said Becky contentedly. "It's perfect."

Becky picked up her telephone, which was also purple, and phoned Ryan. "Come on over," she said to him. "She's here." Becky winked at Althea. "He's having supper with us," she whispered, hand covering the receiver. "He adores you."

Althea lost her breath. It was such an odd feeling, suddenly to have empty lungs and a pounding heart. *Ryan adores me.*

Becky said, "Ryan's going to tell us star stories in the backyard and teach you how to look through a telescope." Becky, laughing wickedly, said, "This whole overnight is a setup, you know."

She opened the kitchen door. A cold wind filtered into the safe warm kitchen. The yard was completely black. Althea grew cold from her feet to her eyes: a deep chill, like an early death.

Becky ran out onto the grass as if entering another, lower world.

Althea cried out. Her breath was gone again, but not from love. Fear yanked it out of her chest. "We — we can't go out there!" she said.

"You afraid of the dark?" teased Ryan, stepping from his yard into Becky's.

Althea hung on to the kitchen counter. "Come back in, Becky!" cried Althea. She smelled the foul eagerness of the vampire.

"Scaredy-cat," Becky teased.

"Make her come back in, Ryan," said Althea desperately. She had to get Becky back inside, in the bright purple bedroom, the safe green kitchen, the many-flowered living room.

Ryan wrapped his arm around Althea. It was an embrace of comfort, not desire. "I don't believe I've ever met anybody who's really and truly afraid of the dark. I'll stay with you. It'll be all right. Think of the dark as a warm and gentle friend."

Althea's laugh rasped like a chain saw.

"I heard something in the bushes," said Becky. "I'll join you two in a minute. I just have to see what it is."

"No!" screamed Althea. "No, you don't! It doesn't matter what it is! Come back in."

"Now, now," said Ryan, holding her, preventing her from saving Becky. I'm in a zoo, thought Althea. Ryan is my keeper.

She felt primitive and savage, felt as if she, like some jungle tiger, had fangs.

Or were her fangs those of a vampire?

It seemed to Althea that it took hours for Becky to return, and that when she came, she moved more slowly. Was paler.

The evening seemed to last for hundreds of years, in which they all grew old and exhausted. She could hardly wrap her mouth around the syllables required for speech. She could hardly see Ryan, could hardly remember Becky.

At last Ryan left.

She adored him, but she could not bear the length of the evening. Every quip, every move, every story consumed her, until all energy was completely sapped. She could hardly unbutton the front of her shirt. She could hardly lift her nightgown. Scarcely brush her teeth. She was actually glad that Becky had turned down the covers of the bed, because she did not know if she could summon the strength to move a blanket.

The mattress was wonderful, so soft, so welcoming, so necessary. The pillow onto which her head sank was a shelter in which she could rest forever. I'll never get up, thought Althea. I'll have to move in with Becky and take a week off from school.

A cold, cruel wind seemed to blow through her mind, filtering through her brain, blinding her eyes.

She'll just be a little . . . tired, the vampire had said.

She was too tired even to shudder.

It can't be, she told herself. I would have felt something. He can't — I mean — those teeth — it wouldn't work unless —

And yet . . . he calls it migration. A word for swallows in the sky. There's nothing in that word about feeling fangs in your flesh.

Be rational, Althea said to herself. Football games, cheering practice. Cheering, studying for exams. Of course I'm tired. I've had a very demanding week.

"Althea, hop up and change the TV channel, will you?" said Becky. "I can't seem to find my remote control."

Althea dragged herself into a sitting position and crawled to the end of the mattress. She could not quite reach the TV knobs. Like an ancient crone with arthritis, she tottered two steps, changed the channel till Becky was satisfied, leaned briefly on the shelves, and pushed herself off like a swimmer pushing off the pool wall for another lap. At last she was back in the bed, back down on the lovely good pillow. Nothing was demanded of her body. Only rest.

Rest.

It was all she wanted.

All she would ever want.

If it's him, she thought, if he was here, with me, I won't have enough energy to have friends. I won't have enough energy to be in the squad or date Ryan or sing in the chorus. Or do anything at all. I'm finished. She said, "Becky?"

"Mmm?"

"When you heard a noise in the bushes, what was the noise?"

"I was just teasing. I didn't really hear anything. I'm sorry if you took me seriously. Ryan was dying to be alone with you outdoors. He had some fantasy that you and he would stare at the stars together, and you would be overcome with uncontrollable emotion, and I would go back in while you two danced in the dark."

In the dark.

Among the hemlocks.

No, she said to herself. It can't be me. He said we were a match for each other. I'm just exhausted, that's all. I've had a hard day. In the morning, I'll be energetic and enthusiastic again.

When Becky found the remote control under a pile of fashion magazines and shouted with delight, Althea slept on, as if in something deeper than sleep.

Chapter 17

But when she awoke on Sunday morning, sun streamed in the bedroom window. It lay golden and warm upon the dark violet of the bedspread and tickled the sweet lavender of the wallpaper.

Althea bubbled with joy.

Nothing had happened. It was cheerleading, and homework, and the pressure of being interesting in front of a new boyfriend that had worn her out. Althea hopped out of bed and went into Becky's darling little bathroom, in which everything was white: white as snow. Shower, tiles, walls, everything gleamed porcelain and pure. Two tiny violet guest towels with lacy fringe hung from a white rod. Violet bath towels were stacked on a white wicker shelf. Embroidered violets peeked delicately from the folds of the shower curtain.

Althea stepped in the shower and sang under pulsing hot water.

She wrapped herself in one of the purple towels

to dry, and the towel was soft and wonderfully thick.

Life is good, thought Althea. I am in control.

She danced into the kitchen to see if she could help with or start breakfast. Becky's parents had apparently come in late, for their bedroom door was shut and the house lay quiet, as houses do on Sunday mornings while people sleep in.

Althea found cereal and milk and crunched happily. Out the kitchen window she could see the backyard, and in the sun it was such a pretty yard. The leaves were gone from the trees, but they were such graceful trees: a willow and two clumps of white birches with papery, peeling bark. The thick shrubs were covered with frost, and they glittered, half snow, half sun, utterly beautiful.

Becky walked slowly into the kitchen. Her eyes seemed to lack focus. Her body lurched slightly, and she sank into a kitchen chair as if unsure where she might be. Althea poured her a glass of orange juice that she had whipped in the blender; it was frothy and light.

Becky looked at the glass. She frowned. She said, "This is so weird, Althea. I just didn't seem to get any rest last night. I don't think I can even pick up that juice glass."

Althea became very still.

Becky said, "I think I'm coming down with something. I don't want you to catch it, Althea. Or Ryan, either. We have such important games next week. He can't get sick; the football team needs him. You can't get sick. The squad needs you."

Through uncooperative, frightened lips, Althea said, "The cheerleading squad needs you, too, Becky. Getting sick is out of the question."

Becky put her arms on the kitchen table and then rested her head on her arms. "I think it's in the question," she said, trying to laugh. "I think — I really think you'd better go on home, Althea. I think I need to go back to bed."

"NO!"

Becky focused one eye on Althea and then closed it, exhausted by the effort. "I feel as if I could sleep for a month," she said.

Althea grabbed Becky's shoulders and shook her. "Get up!" she cried. "You have to get up! You have to try. You have to stay on your feet!"

"Huh?" said Becky, falling asleep.

Becky's mother came into the kitchen. "What's the matter?" she said.

"I think Becky — um — has the flu," said Althea. "She — um —"

Becky's mother went right into action. Thermometer, aspirin, chicken soup, the works. "My poor baby," crooned Becky's mother. "You haven't been sick in years! This is not like you! I think cheerleading is responsible. It takes such time and energy and it is simply draining. I just don't think it's healthy to work so hard day after day, week after week. I've said that all season, haven't I, darling?"

116

"Mmmm," said Becky, leaning on her mother.

With Althea on one side and Becky's mother on the other, they walked Becky back down the hall to her bed, tucked her in, and wrapped her warmly.

"What a sweet girl you are," said Becky's mother to Althea. "So helpful and understanding. I want you to do one little thing for me."

"Anything," said Althea, who felt dead, like something evil and sick, who infected her friends, and ended their happiness. Somebody who could turn a lovely purple-and-white room of irises and violets into a purgatory of exhaustion.

"At practice on Monday, tell Mrs. Roundman that I am taking my daughter off the squad. There is simply too much being demanded of her."

"No!" whispered Althea. "I'm sure Becky will be fine by Monday. She'll be in school Monday. Send a note with Becky to say you want Becky to sit out the practice! Mrs. Roundman will agree to that. Please! Please don't take her off the squad."

Becky had fallen back asleep.

Her long, dark hair swirled on the pillow, like a winter storm cloud around the paleness of her tired face.

My friend, thought Althea. My third betrayal. I have given away Celeste, given away Jennie, and now Becky. Becky!

Her friendship with Becky played in her heart like slides in a darkened classroom: the first welcome, the encouragement at tryouts, the little speech of friendship when she made the squad. The phone calls, the laughter, the hair volume jokes.

I gave her to the vampire.

How many more will I give? When will it be over? Will it ever be over?

Becky's mother kissed her daughter's cheek. "Well," she said, adjusting the blanket hem, "I'll wait till Monday and see. But cheerleading is not worth your health."

Althea no longer knew what cheerleading was worth. She knew only one thing. She was going home. She was closing those shutters, closing them forever, and if it was the end of cheerleading, the end of friends like Becky and boys like Ryan, well, she did not deserve them, anyway.

She felt tight and strong with resolve.

Nothing the vampire could say or offer would make Althea change her mind this time.

She drove over the hills and down to the bottom of the valley.

She parked sternly, with a solid pull on the brake, as if making very, very sure that she was going to stay and see this through. She shut the door of her car not with a slam but with certainty. She strode across her yard, marched up her stairs, and climbed upward.

Chapter 18

The tower room was quiet and dusty in the sun.

It felt of nothing.

There was neither power nor evil here. It was merely an empty room.

She ran her fingers through her hair, as if strengthening herself from the top of her head to the tips of her toes.

She approached the first window. The glass pane lifted quite easily and stayed up. Leaning out of the tower, Althea took hold of one outside shutter.

It was made of wood. Paint flaked off even as she grabbed the rim. The wood felt punky and rotten under her fingers, and when she dug her nails into it, she knew she was leaving half moons of anger in the wood. The shutter whined on its hinges, as if calling out to the hemlocks.

But the sun shone on, and the shutter turned in.

Gripping the shutter with one hand, Althea

reached for its mate. It did not move as easily. She had to lean way far out of the window. She was on her tiptoes now, her center of gravity off, her stance no longer safe.

How high she was.

Below her was not grass, but stone.

Far below.

If someone gave me a push . . . thought Althea. She swallowed, wet her lips, and leaned even farther out, grabbed the opposite shutter, and pulled. It took all her strength to bring the shutters together, but they were only wood, and she was more than that.

Her fingers were cramped and raw from hauling on the splintery, paint-peeling rims, but at last she brought their edges together. She swung the heavy metal clasp on the left shutter and shoved it through the iron circle sticking out of the right shutter like a black wedding ring, and the first pair of shutters was closed.

The louvers of the shutters were fixed, slanting down, and no sun penetrated at that angle.

Now the tower room was darker by a third. The dust seemed to lie more heavily on the floor, and the echo of her footsteps seemed quieter and less important.

Althea turned to approach the middle window. The air in the room thickened and became a wall. She had to lean against it, throw her weight as if against a great invisible wind. Turning sideways Althea hurled herself like a linebacker through the air of the tower room and reached the middle window.

The window refused to lift.

She fought with it. She could jiggle it a little, but not open it.

From somewhere outdoors, through the thin old pane of glass, she heard a laugh, like the sound of dry leaves rustling on pavement.

Althea yelled at him, "Laugh all you want! I'm closing these shutters, and when I'm done with that, you are done, too! You are finished! You are history!"

Like Celeste, thought Althea. Like Jennie. Like Becky. History. They had laughed once. Had fun and friends once. Now they don't.

Well, he had freedom once, because I opened his shutters. And now he won't. So there.

But even so, she was afraid. Afraid of how high up she was. Of how height meant nothing to him. Of what would happen next.

Don't be a weakling, Althea said to herself.

She wrapped her arm in her sweater and punched the window. The glass shattered with a crystalline cry and fell to the stones below. Vicious triangles of windowpane remained in the wood. They glittered in the sun, like vampire teeth.

"You're nothing but glass," Althea whispered to the shimmering fangs. "Nothing but glass."

The window gave up its fight and let itself be lifted easily and quickly.

And the outside shutters, as if not wanting to be

destroyed, submitted to her reaching fingers and let themselves be swung inward, and allowed their clasp and ring to meet, partners forever joined.

The tower room was much darker now. The remaining window faced north. No rays of sun ever came in that window. A little daylight filtered through, but when Althea stood in front of this last window, there was not even enough light to cast her shadow.

It weakened her, as if without a shadow she were without soul as well, without courage and without hope.

After a terrible silent struggle, the third window submitted to her. She did not have to shatter it. For the third time, she thrust her body out to grab a shutter. Leaned way out over the hard stone, tilted dangerously to grasp the wooden rim. The temperature outdoors had dropped severely. She was chilled, her fingers cold to the bone.

These shutters seemed positively eager to close, almost slamming her fingers between them. These shutters want to be shut, thought Althea, and her hair crawled. *Why?* Did the shutters themselves have a scheme in mind? Had they plans? Plans for Althea?

Darkness was deep.

Only the door to the tower room let in any light, and that was from the ceiling fixture in the downstairs hall. She faced the door, trying to gain strength. But it was electric light, manufactured light; it lacked the power of the sun to nourish life; it gave Althea nothing.

That's all right, she thought. I have enough. I will finish this.

She surveyed the tower. The glass was black now, backed with the closed shutters. But there were three more sets of shutters: the inside shutters. And they were the ones that counted.

The chill and the foul-smelling damp that was the vampire swirled around the room, like invisible dervishes spinning, knowing time was up, knowing they would fall to the floor and never spin again.

"I have you now," said Althea. She was triumphant: rich and solid with victory.

She swung the first inside shutter to its closed position.

But it would not go all the way. It resisted. With muscles of its own, it pushed Althea back into the center of the empty room.

The six inside shutters regarded her with their dozens of louvered eye slits.

She threw herself at a different shutter and pushed with all her might. To her surprise it closed without a murmur. She reached for its companion shutter to bring that to the center and bolt them; they were to be coupled by long, thin, black bolts, but when she touched the second shutter, the first returned to its open position against the wall.

Althea's arms were not long enough to reach both shutters at once.

There was no way for her to slide the bolt that would hold a pair down.

The slats of the shutters curved upward into catlike smiles of contempt. *You can't close us*, said the shutters to Althea.

She threw herself at first one shutter and then another, one window and then another — but she could not close a single pair.

A laugh like broken glass spun out of the tower room, through the door, into the hall . . .

. . . and the tower room door, the door that led away from the attic and down the stairs, closed by itself.

Closed tightly and forever.

Her exit was gone.

She had planned to shut the vampire in the tower room.

It had never crossed her mind that he might shut *her* in the tower.

Chapter 19

Althea stood very still.

Nothing but stone, granite, and slate had ever been so still. There was no breath in Althea, no pulse. She was frozen in space and in time.

Is this my choice? she thought. Am I frozen in order to think more clearly? Or because I am so afraid that there is nothing left of me to move?

Her feet were part of the floor, as if nailed to the boards. Her hands hung motionless in the air, as if her bones and tendons had become oxygen and nitrogen.

Or, she thought, has the vampire frozen me? Is this his choice? Is he about to take . . . the next step?

She felt the mold and the fungus of him closing in on her.

What did it feel like?

Would she know when it began and when it was over?

She tried to remember the world. She tried to

think of sunshine and falling leaves, of laughing cheerleaders and peanut butter sandwiches.

How tired Celeste and Jennie and Becky had become. How tired they **had** stayed. Not just their bodies, but their souls, the exhausted skeletal remains of the girls they had been.

Not me, thought Althea. Please, not me!

She knew now that Celeste and Jennie and Becky had felt fear. That they had smelled him, and tasted him, and been sick with nerves from him. She knew now that Celeste and Jennie and Becky had tried to fight back, had put up their hands, as if ten little human fingers could fend off a vampire. She knew now that their hearts had beat with terror, that their lungs had heaved with horror.

I did that, thought Althea. When he said, "They'll just be a little tired," I let myself believe that. I guess you always want to believe that violence will really be gentle. That you aren't really doing anything wrong. That it will all come out happily in the end. Nothing to fret about, especially if you are the winner.

I am the winner, she thought, hysterical with self-loathing. This is what I have won. The chance to be alone with a vampire in a tower of black.

Her thoughts grew as dim as the tower room itself, as if her brain had softened and darkened, and she said to the vampire, *All right. Come in. I accept.*

She felt her hair lift. An odd sort of breeze cooled

the back of her neck. Spin around, she told herself. Raise your fists! Strike out and beat off the attempt.

But something had happened when she closed the shutters. She had closed off a part of herself. All that was strong in her, all that was determined, perhaps even all that was good, had been shuttered away, in some distant and unreachable compartment.

Did I ever have anything good in me? she thought. Will I ever have it again? Or has the goodness of me died inside?

Althea felt movement now, and it was herself.

She was sagging.

Leaning.

Tipping.

I feel awfully tired, she thought.

She yearned to sit. It seemed very important to sit down. Perhaps to lie down.

I need rest, she thought. What time is it? Is it nighttime? Is it bedtime? Is it tomorrow already? Who even cares?

In the tower room, there was no time. There was only dark.

She felt the foil of his fingertips on her skin.

I am letting it happen, Althea thought. I am giving in. It seems that I *have* made a choice. *I have chosen to surrender.*

She tried to see what was happening, but there was nothing to see: nothing but dark . . .

. . . darker . . .

. . . *darkest* . . .

Chapter 20

A horn honked.

A vehicle had pulled into the driveway below.

How twenty-first century! The horn's call pierced the tower room as sunshine could not. Where light cannot travel, sound can.

How beautiful is sound! The driver leaned again on his wheel, and the glorious scream of a car's horn penetrated the tower. No louvers or shutters, no dust, no vampire could stop sound.

Althea smiled into the dark, and immediately the dark was less. A smile, she thought. Happiness. Another weapon. I must remember all these. Sound and joy: They obliterate the enemy.

She straightened. She flung back her hair and opened her eyes wide. It was still dark, but now the dark was curiously friendly. Who had said to Althea that he thought of the dark as a friend?

She waited a moment, hoping her brain would sort out the voices of the week and remember.

Her feet moved; the nails that had held her to

the wooden boards had evaporated. Her hands moved; the paralysis was gone. She walked forward in the dark, encountering nothing, until she touched the wall, and it was only a wall. Plaster. Her hands scrabbled outward until she had found the first window.

Don't drive away, whoever you are, she thought. UPS, FedEx, distant relatives. Stay in the drive.

She lifted the glass without a struggle. The window squeaked slightly, as if relaxing, as if it had wanted to be open. And the iron pins that trapped the outside shutters — they slid up as if just greased. The shutters, too, yearned to swing open.

Throwing them apart, Althea leaned out the window for the second time that day . . .

. . . and it was Ryan.

He's the one to whom the dark is a friend, thought Althea. And now he has saved me from the dark.

Sunshine poured over her, like orange juice from a pitcher. She bathed in its warm yellow liquid. It was so welcome, so delightful, Althea felt as if she could get quite a tan, even though it was winter. She smiled at the sun, and then she laughed, and the vampire was driven away.

"Hey, Althea!" Ryan yelled.

Wait, she thought, don't talk to me yet; I almost understood. It crept partly into my mind. What was it? What did I half know about the vampire and about me?

"Ryan! What are you doing here? I'm so glad to see you!"

"I was just driving by, and I felt this overpowering desire to stop in. You know how it is."

No, I don't know, thought Althea. What overpowered him? What desire was it? "What car are you driving?" she yelled. "It looks like a car with four working doors."

"My father's. I'm running an errand for him. I'm supposed to be getting sandpaper from the hardware store."

"You're miles from a hardware store," she said. I've lost it, she thought. Whatever I nearly understood, I've lost.

"Yup. I'm taking advantage. When you have a car, you have to do your own errands as well. You're in the tower room! Can I come up? I'm dying to see that room."

Not a good choice of words. She shook her head. "Stay there, Ryan."

"Aw, come on, Althea. Why are you so stingy with visiting hours?" He had to shade his eyes to see her.

Stay in the sun, she thought. It's safe in the sun. "It's not night, and you don't have your telescope."

"I always have my telescope!" yelled Ryan, brandishing it. He was not wearing a jacket, although it was cold. She imagined that she could see his muscles under the dark crimson sweater that covered his arms.

Muscles, she thought. What door could stand up to Ryan? He could probably break a lock by turning the handle.

"The sun is shining too brightly, Ryan," she said. "You won't see any stars."

"But I can get oriented," he said, "and figure out what I'm going to see when I do see it."

He could close the shutters.

That was the answer. Together they would shut the vampire out forever. Or in. Whichever it was. What if I do it wrong? thought Althea. What if I accidentally lock the vampire out of doors forever? And he's free to attack forever? I don't know which side of the shutters he has to be on!

The sun vanished beneath a cloud.

The smile on her face was replaced by fear.

The temperature of the wind and the world was lower.

It's dark in this room, she thought, and I have my back to a vampire. "Ryan!" she screamed.

"Haven't gone anywhere," he said, grinning upward.

"Turn on your car radio. Dance for me."

"Do what? Come again?"

"Turn on your car radio! Hard rock! Rap! Techno! Something that hurts the ears."

Ryan was affronted. "It doesn't hurt my ears," he told her. "I love that kind of music."

"Good. Turn it up all the way."

Ryan bent over and leaned inside his father's car, turning the key halfway to get battery power, and the radio surrounded Ryan in a mist of throbbing drums and pounding rap.

Music to scare vampires by, she thought.

Ryan obeyed her. He was dancing. She loved watching him. He hardly moved his feet, but his hips swayed. "Either I get to come up, or you have to come down," screamed Ryan over the blaring music.

We've never danced together, she thought. We'll dance, Ryan and I. We'll dance tonight, and we'll dance tomorrow, and we'll dance our lives away.

"I'll come down," she yelled to Ryan, and knew that she could. The door would open easily when she touched it. She was not trapped; perhaps she never had been, except by her own fear.

She walked out of the tower room and held its door open and looked back in at the grimy shutters and the window she had left open. Wind and rain would come in now, too. But that was all right. Wind and rain were friends, like the dark.

In the hall, under the lamp, she said to the vampire, "So there." She could not see him or smell him, but she knew he was around.

His voice materialized, but not his form. "So you're going dancing?" said the vampire. "Just don't forget who gave you the chance to dance. You owe me."

"I owe you nothing. You took more than you should have."

Althea continued on out of the house, across the porch, down the stairs, and over the gravel. Ryan was still dancing. When Althea reached him, he took her hands and they danced together. Her dancing style was completely different; she flung herself forward, flung herself back, and launched toward him again. They laughed and the music screamed, and he said, "I want to see your tower room."

"No. It really is haunted, and you can't go up there."

Ryan's face split in a delighted grin. "But you can go up? The haunt doesn't bother you?"

"It bothers me on a daily basis."

"Tell you what. I'll go up there and beat it to death."

"Tell you what. We'll drive to Pizza Hut and see everybody."

"Okay. I'm an agreeable-type person."

Ryan finished his dance and slipped into the driver's seat.

Althea finished her dance, circled the car, and put her hand on the shiny chrome handle of the passenger door.

"I like this car," said the vampire conversationally. "Bloodred. It's a nice color."

"Go away," she whispered.

"You want to dance with Ryan?" the vampire whispered back. "Fine. Dance. But every dance is a debt to me."

Chapter 21

Becky was at Pizza Hut!

Althea vibrated like a guitar string. How had this happened? "Becky," cried Althea, "I thought — I mean, when I left this morning, you were — um —"

"Sick as a dog," said Becky cheerfully. "I was whipped."

Althea's head was whirling. She felt like a one-woman roller coaster.

"What do you think was wrong?" asked Kimmie-Jo.

"I don't know, but I had to get well," said Becky simply. "Next weekend is the biggest game of the season, and I'm the one that you and Dusty are throwing into the air and catching during the halftime routine. How could I ruin it by coming down with some dumb flu?"

Ryan said, "It was probably too damp and chilly last night in your yard. We shouldn't have gone outside."

Althea's whole soul felt damp and chilly.

Becky said, "Know what? I swear, when I was dancing around trying to get Althea to come out, the shadows felt like liquid moss."

Kimmie-Jo screamed. "That's so scary," Kimmie-Jo whispered. "Green, wet, shadowy stuff closing in on you?"

I foiled him! thought Althea, exulting. I got her inside before anything happened! I am a match for that vampire!

Becky said, "My mother thinks it's overwork. You wouldn't believe how she carried on. Too much homework, too many papers, too much cheerleading practice, too many hours on the telephone."

Kimmie-Jo nodded. "Probably those hours on the phone. Have some nice nutritious snacks while the other person's talking, to keep your strength up. Cookies or brownies. Then you'll be fine."

Kimmie-Jo seemed completely serious.

"In my family," said Becky, "a nutritious snack is a banana or an apple."

Kimmie-Jo was appalled. "I don't do fruit," she said. "Or vegetables, either."

"But do you do pizza?" said Ryan. "Pizza is always the final solution."

They all cheered for pizza. Althea cheered loudest and longest and she thought: I won. How intrepid I am! I got out of the tower room in spite of the vampire. I saved Becky after all. What power I have. How incredible I am!

Somebody put coins in the jukebox.

"They're playing 'Yellow Fever'" moaned Ryan, as if he had it. "It's my favorite song this week. Althea, dance with me."

"You can't dance in Pizza Hut," said Althea.

"Why not? They put music on, don't they? Do they expect us just to sit here? Of course not." Ryan stood up. Held out his hand.

Before I was popular, thought Althea, I would never have done this. I would have felt like a weirdo and a jerk. I would have been embarrassed. I would have died first.

She and Ryan began dancing between the dark glossy tables while other patrons laughed and watched. She began showing off, which was not natural to her. Ryan was a born show-off.

No, she thought, it's that he was born popular. Popularity all your life makes it possible to dance in the aisles.

Her eyes examined every patron in the restaurant. She saw that popularity, or lack of it, knew no age barrier. There was a little girl, maybe six years old, dancing next to her parents, and that little girl was blond and beautiful, and Althea knew this girl's destiny was to be popular. At another table, children stared enviously but never dreamed of leaving their seats. Two elderly women, alone with their gray hair and wrinkled hands, watched Althea with such sadness that Althea knew they were not remembering their youth when they danced with abandon; they were remembering a youth in which nobody asked them to dance.

I, thought Althea fiercely, will be the one who dances, not the one who yearns. I'm sorry about Celeste and Jennie, but I won't let that happen again, and I'm not giving up what I have.

So there, vampire!

The football team sat in the front of the bus. Every boy wore a jacket and tie and looked both distinguished and uncomfortable.

Ryan's energy overflowed. Twisting in his seat, Ryan yelled back to Althea, lustily sang verses of bus songs, and threw paper airplanes at the coach.

"Ryan," the coach kept saying tiredly, "save it for the game."

"I have more than the game needs."

"Say that when we've won," said the coach.

Althea loved watching the boys when they were apprehensive. Somehow boys never looked as if they got scared. Certainly not football players. It was rather satisfying to know that, yes, they, too, got anxious and tense and tied in knots.

Michael, the best of them, the most athletic, the most capable, was certainly the most nervous.

Since it was an away game, a whole new school's worth of girls would shortly see Michael for the first time. Althea knew well how their eyes would caress and memorize him.

I've always wanted Michael, thought Althea, but now I don't. Isn't that amazing? Michael is such perfection: Every inch of him is splendid. I have had Michael memorized for years. I'll keep him tucked in my mind, something to observe and admire. But not to have.

I like it that he and Constance are a pair.

She looked out the back of the bus. The fan bus was behind them, and she knew Constance was on it; she knew Constance would sit directly behind the cheerleaders, four bleachers up, so that the cheerleaders did not block her view of Michael playing, but so she was still in the thick of the action.

Ryan sent Althea a paper airplane and she sent it back.

How lovely popularity is, Althea thought. It give you choices. If you don't feel like talking, nobody thinks it's because you're such a loser nobody would talk to you, anyway.

You can sort through the boys and girls around you and pick exactly who you want. And with popularity, you have time to know what you want. You aren't taking the dregs or the leftovers. You have the winners, and it's a matter of choosing your own particular winner.

Ryan and two other boys began throwing a pair of sneakers around. The bus driver and the coach yelled, and momentarily the bus stopped by the side of the road while Ryan was informed that responsible young men his age did not behave like that. Ryan seemed interested, but it did not affect him particularly, and the moment the bus was back in traffic, the sneakers were back in the air.

I love him, thought Althea.

The sentence was astounding.

She felt that she must have shouted it out loud, turned it into a cheerleader's cheer, and done it to claps and jumps.

But nobody was looking at her. Not even Ryan.

I love him.

He's mine, and I love him.

O! the life that had been so dark and dreary. Only weeks later, and Althea's life sparkled and glittered like a tiara at a royal dance. She felt that she was composed of diamonds and emeralds, and that Ryan was rubies and sapphires.

Her imagination ran into the future of high school, coursing through dances and yearbooks, committees and clubs. She saw herself with Ryan, wearing jeans and prom gowns, short skirts and Halloween costumes. She saw herself in the cafeteria and the front lobby and the art rooms and at graduation.

Popular.

The boys got off the bus in a unit, sternly ordered (in fact, rudely ordered; the coach had a limited vocabulary and used it often) not to distract themselves by looking at girls. Ryan said, "I'm not going to look at *girls*. I'm just going to look at one. Althea."

He grinned at her, and she laughed back, and the entire cheerleading squad circled her, whispering and giggling and delighted and envious.

Popular.

The game was long and difficult. Once Ryan

was thrown into the mud where he lay twisted and motionless. The coach and the ref ran out to him. But he got up, limped briefly, and was fine. Althea breathed again.

Michael was brilliant.

The sky was blue, the stands packed. The fans had stadium blankets over their legs and scarves around their throats. Pom-poms rustled, and hands clap-clap-clapped. The smell of hot dogs and popcorn filled the air.

Mrs. Roundman said, "You have the right spirit for cheerleading, Althea. That smile never leaves your face. That laugh is so infectious. I would not be surprised if you become captain. You have what it takes."

Chapter 22

The vampire did not appear that night.

He did not appear the following night, nor the night after that.

I got rid of him, thought Althea. I really did it. Oh, wow! I didn't even have to shut the shutters all the way. I just had to get powerful and knock him off the planet.

Althea swaggered a little, laughed some, paraded through the house, and circled the yard, kicking autumn leaves. No laughter like broken glass shattered the peaceful night. Her breath swirled like a dragon's in the cold winter air.

She spent a night at Kimmie-Jo's and went to a party at Dusty's. She and Ryan went to a movie alone together, and another night went with Michael and Constance.

Constance was such a wonderful person. Althea decided to model herself on Constance.

Homework was easy. Quizzes a snap. Teachers admired every word Althea contributed to discussions. Younger girls chose Althea as their favorite cheerleader, and the team won the next game.

The first snow fell.

The dark bleak valley where Althea's house lay turned sparkling white — pure as true love.

She swept the porch and the steps. The snow was dry and tossed in the air like miniature blizzards. The wind blew it back in her face, and she laughed with the joy of living.

It was a night without stars or moon. It was very, very cold.

Ryan, Michael, and Constance dropped her off, and Ryan kissed her good-bye even in front of the others, and Constance said, "See you tomorrow, Althea." Michael tapped his horn good-bye.

Althea stood on the bottom step watching the red glow of their car lights disappear behind the hedge. Ryan was right, she thought. The dark is a friend. When you have friends like I do — like Constance, and Michael, and Ryan, and Becky, and all the rest — all the world is a friend, too.

Through the night came a laugh like sandpaper scraping over skin.

The vampire did not go through the crust. He walked over it, leaving no footprints. The winter wind grabbed his black cape and flung it around him one way and then another, so that he kept wrapping and unwrapping.

The only things that gleamed in the dark night were his eyes and his fingernails. She knew that when he smiled, his teeth would also shine. The crisp clean air turned foul.

The silent night filled with the creaking of shutters, as if they were craning their necks to see the action.

When she shifted position, the snow crackled beneath her boots, as if something were chewing on her ankles.

She was cold, terribly cold, right to the marrow of her bones.

But she said, "I thought you left."

"Briefly. Now I'm back."

"I don't need you," she said. "Go away and stay away."

The vampire stared at her. His jaw dropped in disbelief, and for the first time she saw his tongue. It was pointed and curled up as if rolled in a can. Then he laughed. The pitch of laughter broke the ice that lined the bare branches; the ice fell into the snow below. He said, "You don't need me, Althea? Think again."

She said, "I have thought. And I don't need you. And I won't cater to you. I'm too strong for you, anyhow. I kept Becky safe."

He took a step toward her. She stood her ground. He stank of rot and decay. She gagged. He took another step, and she could not be that close to him. She backed up, and he laughed again. He moved closer to her, she backed up again, he moved again.

"Get away from me," she said fiercely.

"No."

The single syllable was uttered softly this time, and almost regretfully, as if something were about to happen that even the vampire would not enjoy.

This time she dug her boots into the snow and did not let herself back up any more. "I will never again do anything you ask," she said.

He raised his eyebrows. He sucked in his lower lip. The long white teeth inched down toward his chin. They glittered like icicles. They dripped as if melting.

The vampire said, "All right."

To show him that she was completely in control, Althea turned her back. She walked slowly into the house. She shut the door firmly but without slamming it, leaving him in the yard.

She unlaced her boots, knocked the snow off them, and set them on the drying rack.

She unzipped her heavy jacket and hung it in the coat closet.

She took off her scarf, shook the snow away, and looped it around the hanger of her jacket.

The vampire said, "But it will not be all right with you."

Her head jerked up. He was standing on the first step of the stairs. His cape flared out by itself, as if pinned to the walls.

The vampire said, "Go to school tomorrow, Althea. Without me. And see if it is all right. See if you need me. See how strong you are. See if you need to cater to my requests."

She glared at him. "I saved Becky."

"No. The location was too far. My dark path was weak. I could not complete the migration. You had nothing to do with it. Nor did Becky. It was simply an error in navigation and planning."

"You're boring me," said Althea. She thought, I'll just learn to live with it. He'll come by and nag, I'll walk around him holding my breath. Eventually he'll get bored and go back where he came from.

"No," said the vampire. "I am rarely bored. Nor will I go back where I came from. You, Althea, are the one who will go back where she came from. Go back to being invisible. Inaudible. Unloved. Unpopular."

She shrugged.

"Even Ryan will not know your name," said the vampire.

"Get lost," said Althea.

Now he smiled. A smile of joy. The evil crescent covered the entire bottom of his face. "All right. I will get lost. And when you want me back, Althea . . . I may refuse to come."

Chapter 23

In the morning, her car did not start.

Walking was so humiliating. If you couldn't be popular, you should at least have transportation.

But I am popular, thought Althea, smiling. She telephoned Ryan to ask him to ask Michael to stop and pick her up. But Ryan had already left for school.

All right, she told herself. I can walk. One of my friends will see me and stop and pick me up. I'll get teased, but that's okay.

Althea walked to school, up the long, long hill, facing traffic. The cars of high school kids passed her, but no one stopped to give her a ride. No one waved. No one rolled down a window to yell good morning.

The temperature had risen, and the crusty snow had turned to slush. Cars flung black filth on her clothing. Althea stepped in an ice puddle and her boots must have had leaks, because her feet were soaked and painfully cold.

Althea cared deeply about her appearance. She hated people seeing her dirty and wet. I don't even have a car so I can go home and change! she thought.

I'll ask Ryan to borrow Michael's car and take me home, she decided. Or maybe Kimmie-Jo would. Nobody understands the importance of pretty clothes more than Kimmie-Jo.

But nobody noticed the mud on Althea's clothes.

Nobody noticed Althea at all.

Nobody called her name; nobody ran over; nobody registered the fact that she had walked into the school.

Althea went into the girls' room, brushed her hair, and straightened herself up as much as possible. She headed slowly to her locker to hang up her coat, mittens, and scarf.

She was overjoyed to hear her name and turned, laughing, terribly relieved, to see who was calling her.

Nobody was calling her. Two Junior Varsity cheerleaders were striding along behind her. "At least the new season is beginning," said one, giving Althea a look of loathing. "Tryouts for basketball squad will be fair. Unlike the last tryouts."

Althea lost her breath, as if someone had beaten her up. She whispered, "It was fair. I won it."

"It was given to you," said the JV girl. "What experience or background did you have? Huh? Tell me."

"Mrs. Roundman was playing favorites," said the other.

The girls had matching smirks: ugly cruel grasping faces trying to wipe her out of her cheerleading spot.

Althea's cheeks were cherry-red. "May the best one of us make the squad," she said, trying to be a sportswoman.

The girls laughed viciously. "That lets you out. You were no competition for Celeste. And you're no competition for us, either."

Althea clung to her locker, facing the thin metal closet, waiting for the JV girls to pass on. She pressed her hand against the gray door.

A gruesome chill crept up her spine.

How long her fingernails had become. The nails were scarlet and extremely pointed. They were claws. They were inhuman.

Heart pounding, Althea dropped her coat and scarf and dug through her purse to locate an emery board. What could I have been doing to let them get like that? she thought. They looked evil.

And that polish? Althea liked clear polish, or pale pink and slightly glittery. This polish was bloodred.

She could not think clearly. Far from being drained of blood, Althea felt that she had too much. Gallons of blood pounding, throbbing, racing through her veins. Her pulse snapped like drum rims.

The emery board had no effect on the scarlet weapons at the tips of her fingers.

The nails stayed sharp and pointed and . . . toothlike.

Have I become a vampire? With my hands I turned Celeste and Jennie over, and on my hands you can see the proof.

She curled her fingers into fists to hide the evil nails.

A dozen lockers away Becky chattered with Dusty. "I'm really excited about the tryouts, aren't you?" said Becky. "It's always fun to beat the competition."

"Hi, Becky," Althea called. She's my best friend, thought Althea.

Becky looked briefly Althea's way. "Hi," she said without enthusiasm.

Dusty said, "This time we'll get a real cheerleader. It's too bad Celeste is still feeling low. I'd like to see her back. She was fun."

"Didn't we have a great team last fall?" Becky agreed.

Althea struggled with the lock. What was the combination, anyway? She opened her English notebook to the front page where she had scribbled it down on the first day of school. She could hardly remember right from left to make the silly thing turn.

Dusty said, "People who can't even open their lockers are hardly Varsity material."

Althea quivered as if she were Jell-O and somebody had touched her with a spoon. "Becky?" she whispered. "Becky, please — I —"

"Althea," said Becky irritably, "later, okay? I'm busy."

Becky walked away.

No! cried Althea in her heart, in her soul. No! Becky is my friend!

Althea focused on hanging up her coat. She achieved it. She focused on putting her scarf and mittens on the little shelf. She chose the right books to get her through the morning. She said to herself, Becky's moody. It doesn't actually mean anything. I'm okay. It's all still okay.

She wet her lips and took a desperate breath, quieting her fears.

Down the hall came Ryan.

She expanded like a flower in the morning sun: All that was within her turned golden, and when she spoke his name, the syllables were a song of love. Smiles decorated Althea's soul. Joy trembled on her fingertips.

"Hi, Ryan," she said. "I tried to phone you this morning. But you'd already left. I needed you." She laughed a little. Just seeing him made her so happy she had to laugh.

Ryan frowned, as if unsure why she looked familiar. He said, dutifully, as one acknowledging last year's teacher, "Hey, how are you, Althea." It was not a question. It was an anonymous greeting.

He did not care how she was and did not expect her to answer.

"Not too good," she said desperately. "Ryan, I —"

"See you around," said Ryan meaninglessly.

She had turned back into the boring sophomore with the forgettable face and the blank life. Pain like bread knives with serrated edges sawed through Althea's heart.

He walked on and was gone, and the hall was empty.

Life was empty.

She had never believed that *all* her popularity was the gift of a vampire. She would have the popularity she had earned on her own.

But she had been wrong.

She had nothing because she had never been anything. She was just a creation of the vampire.

She thought of skipping class.

She thought of quitting school.

But then she would have to do something else, and what would that be? There were no other lives out there for her. She would have to stagger on through this one.

Althea walked on through the halls, which seemed to widen and lengthen, like a trick to test her commitment to staying alive. She passed the athletic department, and on the wall outside Mrs. Roundman's office was a large sheet of yellow paper with a miniature cheerleading outfit and pompoms tacked to it.

VARSITY CHEERLEADING TRYOUTS
BASKETBALL SEASON
SIGN-UP SHEET

Althea studied the names. She knew them all. There were three times as many as there were positions on the squad. This time there would be real competition. And the girls who had complained that Althea's tryout had been rigged — well, as it turned out, they were proved right, and now had a chance at a fair tryout.

She had pencils in her purse. She could add her name to the list. But why? She could never win on her own. And if she went, she would have to face Becky, and Kimmie-Jo, and Dusty, who would ignore her, or avoid her, or say vaguely, "What's your name?"

And what is my name now? thought Althea. When nobody knows and nobody cares, perhaps you don't actually have a name.

Eventually the morning passed. Eventually the clock turned and it was twelve noon, and time for lunch. Althea was silent amid the screaming hungry students. Althea was slow amid the racing feet of starving sophomores.

She reached the cafeteria last.

All the lines were long.

All the tables were packed.

Except one.

Celeste hunched over a sandwich she was not eating.

Jennie stared down into macaroni casserole she was not touching.

Celeste's eyes were cloudy like an old woman's cataracts.

Jennie's hair, faded and lusterless, fell in her face.

They were at the same table, separated by one chair, unaware of each other.

The chair beckoned to Althea.

Here's your place, whispered the chair. *Here at the table for outcasts. For nobodies.*

Althea tried to leave the cafeteria, but a group of kids came in behind her, and she was tossed forward, like a duck on an ocean wave, closer and closer to the horrible shore of that chair.

Come, said the chair, *sit. You earned this chair.*

Come.

Sit.

Be alone.

Forever.

Chapter 24

Snow has beauty. No matter how deep and troublesome, snow is a blanket of loveliness over a harsh world.

But instead of snow came sleet. Ice-laden rain that pelted down on a slippery gray world. The sky was blotted out.

Kimmie-Jo loaded her car with friends and headed for Pizza Hut. Ryan, Michael, and Constance got in Michael's car. Constance sat in front, between the two boys.

Not one of them called Althea's name.

She walked home in the sleet. Wet ice penetrated her scarf and soaked through her mittens. It was downhill. Twice she lost her balance, slipped, and fell. On the second fall, she tore the knee out of her pants, and her English notebook fell in an ice puddle. The ink ran. The notes were ruined. She sobbed, but no one glanced out of a car window to see.

The towering hemlock hedge around her house

was heavy and sagging with old snow and new ice. Tires from passing cars had flung up grime, so each branch was ugly and stained, like rust.

Althea slipped again on the porch steps. This time when she got up her ankle hurt. She had to haul herself indoors by hanging on to the railing.

I can't try out for cheerleading now, anyway, she thought. My ankle can't bear my weight.

She pulled off her wet clothes and took a long hot bath, surrounding herself with bubbles and perfumes. She wrapped herself in a satiny robe with ivory lace and tucked her feet in soft slippers.

I was going to be captain, she thought. Mrs. Roundman said so. My future is over before it began. My friends have vanished before I even memorized their phone numbers. My cheerleading uniform will be given to another girl, and nobody will remember I was ever on the squad.

She tried to comfort herself with food, but there were no snacks in the house that she could possibly have swallowed. She turned on the television but the laughter hurt her ears. The talk shows were too bright and chatty.

She stood alone in a huge house in a dark valley during a storm.

The phone did not ring.

Other people were gathering for pizza and Cokes. Other people had friends. Other people mattered.

I have algebra to do, she thought. I have to have supper and study for a history test. How can it be that I have a load of laundry waiting? How can it be that I have to open a book, turn a page, sharpen a pencil?

She cried for a long time. She did not feel better. It did not change anything. It just made her eyes red and her head ache.

She went to bed early. There was nothing else to do.

In her dreams a computer tapped out her death knell. Unseen fingers endlessly typed the closing sentences on Althea. The entire world was clicking, tapping, typing. Althea is over, Althea is over, Althea is over.

Althea woke up, cheeks wet with tears, hugging the pillows, because there were no warm bodies to hug and never would be again.

The vampire continued to tap his fingernails on the foot of her bed. The hollow iron frame vibrated with each click. His fingernails were tarnished and yellowy, like teeth that needed brushing. Althea, shivering beneath a stack of heavy wool blankets, wept again.

"You don't have to be alone," said the vampire. His voice was rich and contented, like cream soup.

Or blood.

She looked at him through her tears. He was not wearing his cape. He seemed almost not there; he was mostly voice and fingernails.

Where's the rest of him? she thought, swiveling eyes and head like an owl, afraid to turn her back, but needing to locate the enemy.

"I'm sorry you had to suffer today," said the vampire. "Sometimes lessons are painful to learn. Have you learned your lesson, Althea?" the vampire asked.

She held the pillow in the air between them.

"You may have it back now, if you're a good girl," said the vampire.

"Have what back?" said Althea weakly.

His voice whispered through the room like a cat purring. "Popularity," he breathed. The cape appeared. It leaned past the vampire's shoulders toward Althea, and this time its edges were velvet and rich.

"No," she said. The velvet cape settled on the edge of the bed and tucked its edges around her feet to warm them.

"You must keep Becky," the vampire said. "You need a friend. Becky will be your friend."

Oh, to have Becky back as a friend! To have the phone ring, laughter ring, a friend's voice ring!

Althea buried her face in the pillow.

"You give me Constance," said the vampire. His cape was as furry as a teddy bear. *Wear me,* it said silently.

Althea pulled her feet up closer to her chest and tucked herself into a little round ball, as far from the cape and the vampire as she could get.

"Constance," repeated the vampire.

Give him Constance? Who was perfect? Who was right for Michael? Who with Michael made a couple she loved?

"You'll make the basketball squad," said the vampire. "You'll be busy and happy, surrounded by friends."

Constance?

"Ryan will be waiting for you after tryouts," said the vampire. "He feels terrible that he was rude today. He cannot imagine why he acted like that."

She had no lights turned on, and yet the bedroom had a strange sheen. Pink walls, peach carpet, quilted chair — all glowed.

"A new captain will have to be elected," whispered the vampire.

She trembled.

"The most popular girl is always chosen captain," whispered the vampire. "You will be the most popular girl."

She stared at the lace edge on the pillowcase. How pretty it was. How fragile and how feminine. She touched it with her fingers. Her cruel scarlet talons nearly tore the lace. She pushed them back under the blankets. I want ordinary fingernails, she thought. Soft, rounded, pink nails.

"I would never make another request after Constance," said the vampire silkily. "You need only bring Constance into my dark path."

She would be popular again. A cheerleader again. Have friends again. Have Ryan again.

"Only Constance?" she whispered.

Their voices matched: airy and bodiless. Light

and frothy. As if they were talking of nothing. Just feathers and dust.

"Constance," he repeated. The vampire smiled. She found that she had become accustomed to his smile. There was a certain symmetry to the way his teeth lined up that other smiles did not share.

"Never anybody else?" she whispered.

"Of course not," he assured her.

She laughed bitterly. "You're lying."

He smiled. His teeth chattered. They pecked at his lip like the beaks of birds. The teeth clicked up and down; his fingernails clicked up and down; and the typing typed out, *Second chance, Althea, second chance! Just Constance, just Constance!*

"I won't be back again," said the vampire. The cape slithered off her bed. "Either you take this chance, Althea, or you do not. Either you are popular again, or you are not. It's quite simple, really." The cape tightened around the vampire like a cocoon shutting in a dying butterfly. "Now get a good night's sleep, Althea. Tomorrow is an important day for you."

She shut her eyes.

When she opened them he was gone.

She was alone.

And that was the decision, really. Not Constance. But whether she could stand to be alone for the rest of her high school life. Unloved. Unwanted. Unspoken to.

Chapter 25

Her car still would not start. But she had scarcely reached the sidewalk when Kimmie-Jo honked a horn, pulled over, and shrieked, "Althea! You can't walk in this weather! Get in! Why didn't you call me and say you needed a ride? You silly. You'll catch cold."

Althea rode to school with the captain of the cheerleading squad. Kimmie-Jo talked of boys and cheers, got the best parking space in the student lot, and danced alongside Althea as they entered the lobby. "I just love it that you're going with Ryan," she confided. "You and Ryan, and Constance and Michael, you're such adorable couples! The whole school is crazy jealous of you, Althea."

Some girl changing the Artwork of the Week shouted, "Hi, Althea!"

Some boy pushing a cart of audiovisual equipment said shyly, "Hi, Althea, how are you?"

Becky bounded over. "Althea, are you ever going to forgive me?" she said.

"For what?" said Althea, smiling. How pretty Becky was! How cute and bunny-rabbitlike she looked, her nose twitching in anxiety.

"For being nasty yesterday," said Becky, hanging her head. The ponytail fell sadly on her shoulder. "I don't know what came over me! I sat there at Pizza Hut and felt like the creep of the century. Don't be mad."

"I'm not mad," said Althea. "We're friends." *You need a friend. Becky will be your friend.* I have her for good, thought Althea. She will always be my friend.

Becky said, "Ryan won't see you till fifth period, so he asked me to give you this note." It was a sheet of notebook paper folded six times, until it was a fat cube the size of a thumb. *Yesterday was out of control. Sorry. Really, really, really sorry. Are we still friends? Love, Ryan.*

Kimmie-Jo said, "I love notes. I see Ryan next period, Althea. I'll take the answer to him. No fair folding it up so I can't read it."

They all laughed. Althea wrote with a great flourish, *Friends forever. Love, Althea.*

School flew by. Never had those fifty-minute class hours seemed so short. Never had lunch been such fun.

Ryan sat with her, of course. Settled down very close, so her wool skirt rubbed against his corduroy pants. His bright eyes were only inches from hers. He said, "I didn't know how much fun it is to be with you till yesterday when you weren't around." He blushed. He said, "I'm not letting that happen again."

Outside, the sky lightened and turned blue again, and the sun actually shone, melting the snow that had sealed the skylights. Yellow and gold filtered through. Ryan asked her to go with him to the Winter Formal.

Nobody had ever asked her to a dance before.

Michael said, "Constance and I are going, of course. Let's the four of us go together. Would you like to do that, Althea? Maybe we could have dinner out before the dance. Constance loves elegant restaurants. She'll go anywhere if she can get really dressed up."

Two tables away, Jennie sat alone, pushing macaroni around on a lunch plate until it turned cold. Celeste tried to sit with old friends, but they scorned her, elbowed her away, and Celeste, sad and limp, sat with Jennie after all.

Althea averted her eyes.

After school, at her locker, Ryan, Michael, Dusty, Kimmie-Jo, and Becky gathered. There was a heavy argument going because some people did not want pizza today, but were in hamburger moods. There was even a holdout for fried chicken.

"You decide, Althea," said Michael. "We'll follow you."

The boys stood on each side of her. Althea drank in their good looks, their smiles, their attention. My locker, she thought. My locker is where the best people meet.

Ordinary kids slipped by, pressed against the far wall, so as not to disturb the popular crowd. Some kept their heads low, to avoid notice; others were brave and stared longingly at Althea and her friends.

Celeste was in the first group.

Celeste paused to rest, leaning against the wall. She did not look as if she remembered the cheerleading crowd, and they certainly took no notice of her. Celeste fastened her eyes at the far end of the hall, planning the long journey. She picked up first one foot, and then the other, trudging on.

Constance flew toward them.

Everybody shouted, "You're late, Constance! Where've you been?"

Michael held out his right hand and still running, she clasped it, so that they both swung a few feet, till her momentum was stopped. Then they smiled secrets into each other's eyes and laughed a little.

Althea's hands turned as cold as deep water in ancient lakes.

"Hi, Althea," said Constance, smiling warmly. "We missed you yesterday."

Althea's nerves felt as if somebody were stitching needles through her skin. "Thank you," she said.

"You know what?" said Constance.

"What?" said Althea. She was out of breath. Her lungs had shrunk. She could not squeeze another molecule of air into them.

Constance put her arm around Althea's waist and gave her a slight squeeze. "You add so much when you're around, Althea."

Somehow the four of them were walking together in one straight line: Michael, Constance, Althea, Ryan. Althea felt like royalty. As the foursome passed, heads turned. People stopped talking, turning, or lockering, and feasted their eyes on the two couples.

Constance said, "Do we have to join everybody else again today? Sometimes I get so tired of the crowd. Let's go somewhere, just the four of us, and get to know one another better." She smiled, just for Althea.

It's me she wants to get to know better, thought Althea. She wants us to be friends.

"I'm still waiting to be allowed to use my telescope in your tower room, Althea," said Ryan. His hand left hers briefly to touch her hair. He seemed almost in possession, as if it were his hair now.

They reached Michael's car. Michael and Constance sat in front. Ryan and Althea sat in back.

"Well?" said Michael, turning the key in the ignition. "Where are we going? Up to you, Althea. What's your command?"

Don't do it, she said to herself. Remember Jennie and Celeste. How pitiful they are. Don't do that to Constance! She's a nice person. She wants to be your friend. Don't do it to Michael! He loves Constance. There won't be a Constance left to love if you bring her into the dark path.

But I have to, she thought. I can't have a life as lonely and worthless and dreary as last night. As the first year of high school. Nobody deserves that kind of life! I deserve friends and happiness!

"I have to make a turn at that red light," said Michael, tossing a smile back over the seat to Althea. "So you have to issue instructions before then."

If you give him Constance, you'll have betrayed a third friend!

If you don't give him Constance, you'll never have a friend again.

Althea hung tightly to Ryan's hand. She said, "Let's go over to my house. There's plenty to do there. Plenty to eat."

"And tower rooms to go in," said Ryan, delighted, squeezing her hand back.

"And tower rooms to go in," said Althea.

Constance clapped her hands. "I missed your party," she said, "and I felt so left out. Do I get to go up in the tower, too?"

"Of course," said Althea.

Chapter 26

The valley road was as low and empty as a back alley. No cars except Michael's passed through its darkness. "It's always winter on this part of the road," said Constance uneasily. She shifted position in the front seat, playing with the shoulder belt.

"What's the matter?" Michael asked her.

"It's spooky." Constance was shivering. "Aren't you ever afraid, Althea?" Constance pulled her coat around herself and buttoned the toggles.

She feels it, thought Althea. The dark path has already touched her, and somehow she knows something is wrong. She's trying to protect herself.

Constance said, "The hemlocks circle the house, don't they? Like a castle gate." Constance tried to laugh. She pointed toward the outer edge of hemlocks, which formed a dark needled tower of their own.

"Double towers," said Ryan, grinning. Nothing

had touched him. There was nothing out there but boring old trees.

"The tips of the hemlocks are waving at me," said Constance.

Michael said, "Constance, you're not usually so poetic. Next you're going to tell me you see ghosts flitting in the shadows." The boys laughed.

Constance said, "I do see something."

"It's the wind," said Ryan.

"If I lived here," said Constance, "I'd be afraid of everything always."

They were half a block from the blackness of loneliness that would enclose Constance forever once she left this bright and shining car.

Constance won't be the last one, thought Althea. The vampire was lying. He'll have to have more. I'll have to give them to him. That will be my life. Choosing his next victim. That will be who I am. The vampire's procurer.

She sank back into Ryan's arms, trying to find comfort.

But there was no hiding from the decisions she had made.

All I wanted was to be a cheerleader! To have the phone ring! To have friends! Was that so terrible? Was I so wrong?

They were only a car length away from her driveway. The cruel green hemlocks had reached down to meet them. The branches seemed to curl their tips in greeting.

It *was* terrible, she thought. I *was* wrong.

Her heart had enlarged. It was bursting with pain. She tried to hate the vampire. But the vampire was not half so important as she was. She hated herself.

I am loathsome. Human beings do not do to one another what I have done.

Even if I save Constance, that won't balance it out. Because I can never save Jennie or Celeste. They're gone. So what's the point in ruining everything? I paid so much to purchase popularity!

You can't un-pay, thought Althea. When you've done a terrible thing, it's there, forever and ever.

Since that's true, why shouldn't I keep my popularity forever and ever? What difference would it make to Jennie and Celeste?

Constance began twining a lock of hair in and around her fingers, nervously looking out into the shadows.

It would make a difference to Constance, thought Althea.

Althea thought of lonely cafeterias and silent phones.

She said calmly, "Turn around, Michael."

"Huh?" Michael kept on driving.

"I'm starving. Let's get pizza after all," explained Althea.

"I've bought you plenty of pizza," protested Ryan. "You owe me a tower."

"No," said Althea. "Don't go in my driveway, Michael."

It was too late. Michael had already turned into the driveway.

"Back up!" screamed Althea. She leaned over the seat and took hold of Michael's shoulders and shook him. "Get out of here!"

Michael stopped the car, rear wheels in the street, front wheels in the driveway. Hemlocks reached down all around them, trying to move them forward, coaxing them another few feet.

"Althea, you're so sweet," said Constance. "I'm being silly, afraid of a dumb old hedge. It's okay, Althea. I want to go to your house. Really. Don't pay any attention to me." Constance tapped the steering wheel. "Drive on in, Michael."

"No," whispered Althea. "I'm not inviting you after all."

Michael and Ryan stared at her, appalled. But Constance said, "Let's hop out here. Let's walk the rest of the way." She put her hand on her door handle.

Althea thought of Constance drained and stupid. Of Constance dulled and trudging. She thought of Constance, ignored and unloved.

"No!" screamed Althea. "Don't get out of this car!"

Now she was gripping Constance's coat as well as Michael's.

"This is a wrestling match?" said Michael politely. "Althea, what's the matter with you?"

Ryan said tightly, "She doesn't want me around,

do you, Althea? That's what this is about, isn't it?" His handsome face was marred by hurt and confusion. "You just plain don't want me at your house."

There must be a way to have it all, thought Althea. Surely, I can have friends *and* foil the vampire. There must be a way to hang on to my friends! I'll have thought up some excuse for this by the time we reach Pizza Hut.

"Fine," said Ryan. "You go to your precious tower, Althea. We'll go somewhere else." He yanked Althea's hands off Michael and Constance and leaned across Althea's lap and opened her door. He pointed to the driveway.

Althea laughed hysterically and stepped out of the car. The vampire was going to take away her popularity right now. She would not even get as far as Pizza Hut.

Ryan said to Michael, "So do what the lady says. Back up and drive away." Ryan slammed the door behind her.

Althea stood in the slush. The valley lay chilled and quiet. It was like being in a gutter, with dead leaves and torn newspaper tangling around her ankles.

Michael's car backed up. Michael's car drove away. Constance was safe.

Althea walked to her house without looking back.

The branches of the hemlocks leaned down to meet her, and the dark needles of the hemlocks closed behind her.

Hope was gone.

Chapter 27

Exhaustion unlike anything she had ever known tormented Althea. The steps up the porch were like mountains. The scale of everything had changed: She was a tiny child now, and these were the stairs of a giant.

I did the right thing! she thought, weeping. I saved Constance! Why didn't I get to keep my friends when I was good at last?

The vampire met her on the top step.

The symmetry of his teeth was hypnotic. The points of two of them were as piercing as pencil tips, fresh from the sharpener.

"An interesting choice," said the vampire, his voice as level as a lily pad on still waters. "Your cheerleaders will laugh at you. Your football player will forget you. You do have, you know, a forgettable face."

Althea opened her purse and took out her mirror. In its little square she studied this forgettable part of her body. Although the vampire stood directly behind her, when she tilted the mirror, he did not show in the glass. He has no reflection, she thought. And I, in the morning, will have no reflection, either. Nobody will know my name or face.

"As for me," said the vampire, "I, too, have made a choice."

She closed the plastic cover on the little purse mirror and put it away. There would be no need to use it again; it would never again matter how she looked.

His voice was sticky, like spiderwebs. "You are no longer a match for me, my dear."

I'm his dear, she thought. I catered to him and pandered to him. You know how low you've fallen when you are dear to a vampire.

The vampire touched her chin and lifted her face to look at him. He had never touched her before. It was as spongy as she had expected, as if he were swollen with rot beneath his skin.

"It is time, my dear," said the vampire.

"Time for what?" said Althea dully. She had no time that mattered anymore. Nobody was waiting for her or interested in her.

"For us," said the vampire. He swept his cape around her shoulders, and they walked together in its black velvet. The foul smell of him was intoxicating. She gagged, but she wanted more of it, and she breathed deeply.

He said, "Just a few steps to negotiate, my dear."

She took his hand. His fingernails, wrinkled and tarnished like old foil, glittered against her fair skin.

He said, "I do so love the view from the tower, don't you, my dear?"

She said, "Are you migrating? Is that what is happening?"

"Of course, my dear. You're just going to feel a little tired afterward."

Althea nodded. She said, "I'm not arguing with you. I thought I would argue with you. There was that time I threw chairs at you."

"You welcome my presence. You are eager. You thought you were saving Constance, but that's not really the case. You wanted to be here yourself, Althea. You wanted to be part of the migration."

Althea's mind drifted. "Like robins?" she asked. "Like swallows?"

The vampire smiled. His curly pink tongue ran wetly around his thin lips and stroked his teeth. "Not quite. There, Althea. We've reached the landing. Another few steps and we'll be at the tower door."

The vampire's face was all teeth. Sharpened at the ends like pencils.

"You said you would make me popular," Althea said.

"And you had a good time, didn't you, my dear? Being popular was quite wonderful, wasn't it?"

Althea stumbled.

The vampire said, "This is the last step, Althea."

He drooled over the words. "The very last step you ever have to take," he whispered.

The very last step, thought Althea.

But it's not the last step that matters. It's the first step.

If I had not taken the first step, I would not be here now. I brought him Celeste. It is fitting that I should surrender to him now and become like Celeste and Jennie. I deserve it. "Does our original agreement stand?" asked Althea.

"I suppose it does," said the vampire, "although that hardly matters now. Come, my dear, let's open the tower door together."

"What happens," said Althea, trying to lift her foot up that last step, trying to go with him, "after me?"

"There are others," said the vampire. "Girls who don't matter. Girls without friends. Girls who will do whatever I ask." He smiled hugely. "Girls like you, my dear."

"Who want to be popular?" said Althea.

The vampire nodded and bent over to help lift her foot over the final barrier.

Althea's voice became a whimper. She said, "I want to be popular one more time. Please? Please, please, please?"

The evil crescent of the vampire's smile covered his face.

"Because if I could be popular just one more time . . . " She begged, she groveled, she whined. "I would remember it," she sobbed. "I would frame it in my mind and keep it. I would make it last. Like an ice-cream cone. I would have it slowly. I would know how wonderful it is."

"Like an ice-cream cone," repeated the vampire, laughing. "Licking the edges, trying not to let it drip away from you." He licked his lips in a circular motion.

"Please?" she sobbed. "Please let me be popular one more time."

The vampire paused. He looked around the house, the house from which neither she nor he could ever escape. He opened the tower door. It creaked when it swung. The tower room was frigid. The window she had left open when Ryan parked in the driveway had a rim of ice on it. He looked at Althea, clinging to his hand, begging, begging, begging, for one more gift.

"Well . . . " said the vampire.

"I'll do anything," she said fervently. "I'll do anything."

The vampire laughed again. "I know, my dear. You always have."

She clasped her hands. "Then I can have my popularity one more time? I can sit with Ryan? And Becky? And Kimmie-Jo? And Michael? I can cheer in one more game?" A desperate tremor of a smile, a hideous facsimile of a smile, spurted across her face like a wound.

"Hold out your arms, Althea," said the vampire.

She held them straight out, like tree branches.

He gave her an invisible burden, spread on her

extended arms and palms as if she were carrying a freshly ironed gown. "Your popularity," he breathed. "As invisible as you will be in the morning."

The popularity was invisible, but it warmed her, the suntan of friendship. She could hear the voices of friendship: distant laughter and remote chatter. It caught her up, like traffic, rushing her down the halls, tossing her among the best crowd.

I did anything to get you, she thought. I destroyed myself to have you. I'm going to do it again, too.

A cold draft from the tower passed through the popularity, turning it as autumn winds turn leaves.

It awakened her slightly, as chilly winds do, and she looked up and into the tower.

The shutters will stay open, she thought. Long after I have sunk like Jennie and Celeste. The vampire's dark path will cross the hemlocks, and slip through the trees, and find others. Other girls who want to be popular. Who are weak.

I am going down, thought Althea. But I will *not* take another girl with me. I will take *him*. There will be nothing left of me. But instead of the popularity one last time, I will have the vampire. It will be his last time.

Resolve — warmer, hotter, sterner than popularity — filled her heart, and mind, and soul. "I reject your gift," said Althea softly. "I'm getting rid of it."

"You can't do that," said the vampire.

Althea smiled. The smile inched down her body, giving her strength, first to her face, then to her shoulders, her heart, her arms.

The vampire's teeth went back into his mouth. He looked alarmed.

"That's your source of power, isn't it?" she cried. "When weak people take what you offer, you become strong. You would have had no power if I had had the courage to ignore you." Strength from understanding crept down into her legs. Althea kicked his black cape away and stomped on it. She began laughing.

The vampire took a step backward into the tower room.

"I won't let you do it to others," said Althea. "I won't let you lay out any more dark paths."

The vampire held up his hands to stop her. She smacked them out of her way.

"No!" said the vampire. "You can't do this!"

Rhythm unbroken, feet unstoppable, Althea stomped toward the vampire. As she advanced, he backed up.

"You are nothing! And I am a match for you!" Althea cried.

The vampire kept moving back.

She leaped forward. The vampire hunched over into a ball, like a porcupine hiding its soft underbelly. Althea grabbed him. She took her popularity and pushed it against him, shoved it on him, wiped it on his face and his clothes. She mopped him with it.

"There," she said. "It's yours again."

His speech changed. He no longer sounded human. He no longer spoke English. A whimpering babble spurted from his mouth. His sharp teeth hung over the edges of his thin lips like foam.

"I'm free," Althea said.

She smiled. Not at the vampire, nor the world, nor a handsome boy, but at herself. She was free. That deserved a smile.

Efficiently she snapped the shutters together. The shutters that had rebelled when she was weak surrendered now that she was strong.

The vampire was trapped by the shutters that bound him, like lids on coffins.

She left the tower. The door locked by itself.

For a while, the vampire beat on the floor and on the door, but he had no power without a victim. Eventually the noise stopped.

I have stopped him, thought Althea. But what matters more, I stopped *myself*.

She walked down the stairs. Walked out of the house. Walked into the yard, in the sleet and the ugly dark. There were no threats. There was only weather and winter.

I have no friends. I will have to make friends the way other people do, one at a time, by being nice. I am not a cheerleader. I will have to get on the squad the way other girls do, by practicing hard.

Someday I will have it back.

But I will have earned it.

It will be mine, and I will *never* have to give it away.

I will deserve it.

The house is still there, although Althea moved away. The hemlocks are taller, thicker, and darker. When night falls, cars do not drive by and strangers keep their distance.

Two winters have damaged the tower. One of the shutters has come loose. It's banging against the tower, as if something inside hopes to get out.

The house is for sale.

It will appeal to somebody with children, somebody who needs plenty of space. One of the children might become curious about the tower. Play with the shutters.

And find a vampire.

A vampire who needs a victim.

A vampire who is used to waiting. And winning.

About the Author

CAROLINE B. COONEY has written nearly seventy books for young people, including *Freeze Tag, Fatality,* and The Losing Christina trilogy: *Fog, Snow,* and *Fire.* Her books have sold over ten million copies and been printed in many languages. She lives in Connecticut with three pianos, two computers, and lots and lots of books.

Vampire's Promise #2:

EVIL RETURNS

Devnee is tired of being ignored. Tired of feeling
ordinary. All she wants is to be beautiful. If she's
beautiful, everything else will fall into place: popularity, friendship, even love.

Devnee's family has just moved into a new
house — a house with a vampire in it. He can grant
Devnee's wish, but there's a price. Is she willing to
pay it?

Vampire's Promise #3:

FATAL BARGAIN

Lacey and her friends just want some fun. And what could be more fun than spending the night in a creepy old house? Especially a creepy old house with a strange circular tower? It's all just harmless fun, right? Wrong!

A vampire lives in that tower, and he wants something before he'll let them leave. One of them will have to stay . . . and there's only one more catch. Lacey and her friends must choose the person who has to stay behind.

And don't miss Caroline B. Cooney's
compelling trilogy

Losing Christina #1:

FOG

You can get lost in the fog.
In the fog things can happen that no one sees.

Mr. Shewington, the handsome principal, Mrs.
Shewington, the dedicated teacher. Who better for
Christina and Anya to board with while attending
school on the mainland?

But something evil is happening at the Shewingtons' house. Anya is slowly losing her mind,
and Christina knows that the Shewingtons are behind it.

Now they are turning their attention to her.

"You don't know yourself, Christina," they tell
her. "You cannot admit that you are a very dis-
turbed child."

SNOW

Outside, she could freeze.
Inside, she could die.

Everyone says Mr. and Mrs. Shewington are lovely people.

But Christina knows otherwise. She sees what they are doing: First, they chose Anya. Then Christina — but Christina was too strong for them. . . . So now it's Dolly, sweet, trusting Dolly.

Poor Dolly. Everyone thinks she is outside somewhere, lost in the snowstorm.

But Christina knows Dolly isn't outside. She's inside. Lost somewhere in the Shewingtons' house. And that's much worse.

Losing Christina #3:

FIRE

They say Christina likes to
play with fire. Fire is dangerous.

Finally, Christina has evidence.

She has found the Shewingtons' files.

The files they reread lovingly, together, at night.
The files on the empty-eyed girls in mental hospitals across the country. Girls they have destroyed.

But now the files are evidence. The Shewingtons will have to get rid of the evidence — and Christina.

This time they'll use fire.